"I came for a drink of water."

"Come on in." Dori pulled a glass out of the cupboard, filled it at the sink and handed it to Eli.

"*Danki.*"

She gifted him with a smile. "*Bitte.* How's it going out there?"

He smiled back. "Fine." He gulped half the glass then slowed down to sips. No sense rushing.

After a minute, she folded her arms. "Go ahead. Ask your question."

"What?"

"You obviously want to ask me something. What is it? Why do I color my hair all different colors? Why do I dress like this? Why did I leave? What is it?"

She posed all *gut* questions, but not the one he needed an answer to. A question that was no business of his to ask.

"Go ahead. Ask. I don't mind." Very un-Amish, but she'd offered. Insisted.

He cleared his throat. "Are you going to stay?"

She stared for a moment and then looked away. Obviously, not the question she'd expected, nor one she wanted to answer.

Mary Davis is an award-winning author of more than a dozen novels. She is a member of American Christian Fiction Writers and is active in two critique groups. Mary lives in the Colorado Rocky Mountains with her husband of thirty years and three cats. She has three adult children and one grandchild. Her hobbies are quilting, porcelain doll making, sewing, crafts, crocheting and knitting. Please visit her website, marydavisbooks.com.

Books by Mary Davis

Love Inspired

Prodigal Daughters

Courting Her Amish Heart
Courting Her Secret Heart
Courting Her Prodigal Heart

Love Inspired Heartsong Presents

Her Honorable Enemy
Romancing the Schoolteacher
Winning Olivia's Heart

Visit the Author Profile page at Harlequin.com for more titles.

Courting Her Prodigal Heart

Mary Davis

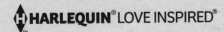

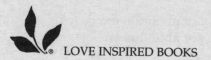

LOVE INSPIRED BOOKS

Recycling programs
for this product may
not exist in your area.

ISBN-13: 978-1-335-47889-4

Courting Her Prodigal Heart

www.Harlequin.com

Printed in U.S.A.

It was meet that we should make merry,
and be glad: for this thy brother...
was lost, and is found.
—*Luke* 15:32

German Proverb

Mer sott em sei Eegne net verlosse;
Gott verlosst die Seine nicht.

One should not abandon one's own;
God does not abandon His own.

To my son Josh

Chapter One

Goshen, Indiana

With the reins in hand, Eli Hochstetler drove his *vater*'s supply-hauling wagon through Goshen in the early-June sun. Dutch's hooves clip-clopped on the pavement.

Daniel Burkholder sat on the seat next to him. "Have the church leaders given you permission to purchase a computer and make a website?"

Eli shook his head. "I haven't asked yet."

"Why not? The summer is going to be over before you know it."

"I need to have more items made first." Eli had branched out his blacksmithing from the practical horseshoes, weather vanes and herb choppers to decorative items like napkin holders, door knockers and small animal figures. This second group of items would be marketed toward *Englishers*, hence the need for a computer and website. Not everyone who requested such privileges were granted them.

"Shouldn't you make sure they'll let you before you go to the trouble?"

"I want to show them I have a need and *meine* work can support a business. I also need to learn about websites and such."

"You can't create your own website. They wouldn't allow that. You'll need an *Englisher* to do that."

"I know. I'm not sure how to go about finding one."

"Doesn't every *Englisher* know about computers?"

Eli shrugged. "I think so. If I know a little, I'll know how to talk to an *Englisher* about *meine* website."

His attention gravitated toward Rainbow Girl. That was what he called the young woman with rainbow-colored hair. His gaze automatically followed her.

For the past six months, he'd seen this same girl every time he came to town, without fail. Her multicolored hair made her hard to miss, but she held herself differently today. Not the usual bounce in her step. Not the usual head held high. Not the usual carefree swing of her arms. Her head hung low, and her shoulders hunched over. Her fancy black knee boots scuffed the sidewalk, and her body shook as though she was crying.

What drew him to this stranger? An *Englisher*, no less. It made no sense.

Inasmuch as ye have done it unto one of the least of these my brethren, ye have done it unto me.

Ne, this verse didn't apply.

Not for an *Englisher*. Therefore, not his responsibility. And none of his business.

"You aren't going to ask *her* for help, are you?"

Daniel's question brought Eli back to his right

mind. "Of course not." He snapped the reins to hurry up Dutch. He had errands to complete and work to do.

"What is it about that *Englisher* that makes you stare?"

Eli shook his head. "I don't know what you mean."

"The last three times I've ridden into town with you, you've watched her. You don't do that with other *Englishers*."

Eli hadn't realized he'd been so obvious. "Who wouldn't notice someone with hair like that? You've obviously noticed her also."

"That's different. You stare like you're trying to figure her out." Daniel's assessment was too accurate.

Eli struggled to figure out what drew him to this one *Englisher*. He didn't want to talk about her anymore. "We should get the lumber first, then the feed."

A while later, with his errands done and the wagon loaded down, Eli drove back through town. Would he see Rainbow Girl once more? He hoped not. He didn't want Daniel bringing her up again.

But there she sat. Alone. Huddled on the curb in front of a sandwich shop with her arms wrapped around her bent legs.

He guided Dutch into the small strip mall parking lot, pulled the draft horse and wagon through two adjoining spaces and hauled back on the reins.

Daniel elbowed him. "What are you doing?"

"I'll be right back." After setting the brake, he jumped down and headed toward Rainbow Girl.

He hesitated a few feet away. What did an Amish man say to such a person?

One side of her hair had been cropped very short while the other side hung down to her shoulder. The short side shone bright red, and her ear had *five* ear-rings. Purple bangs swooped across her forehead and partially covered one eye. Then came sections of blue, green, yellow, orange and around to the red again. All of it had about an inch of brown close to her head. Why would anyone do that to her hair?

Her jeans had several large holes up and down the entire fronts in various sizes. With her legs bent, her black-net-covered knees poked out the biggest open-ings. A green army-style jacket hung loose over a baggy T-shirt.

Englishers were strange.

His heart raced being this close to her after all these months and now contemplating speaking to her. He should leave, but instead, he said, "Are you all right?"

Slowly, her head rose, and she stared at him as though she'd seen something out of the ordinary. Per-haps she had. Amish didn't normally talk to *Englishers* like her.

Her lips were purple, similar in color to the hair that covered part of her face. Above her upper lip sat a dot of silver metal. She had a small silver hoop hanging from the one eyebrow he could now see. Heavy black makeup encircled her eyes as though she'd used soot. Below them, the black had run and smeared. Why did *Englisher* women choose to cover up their beauty with so much paint?

"I'm fine. Leave me alone."

All her makeup couldn't disguise the pain in her eyes. Pain that came from deep inside. From her heart and soul. "You don't look fine." There must be some-thing he could do. Why he felt a need to help her, he didn't know. He pointed to his own face. "Your eye… The black stuff… Never mind."

She wiped her fingers below each eye, further smearing the inky mess. "I'm fine."

This woman obviously didn't want anything to do with him. He shouldn't bother her any longer. He should leave. Instead, he sat on the curb near her, keeping a respectable distance, at least four feet. He glanced toward Daniel, who shook his head.

Eli needed to make sure she was all right. "My name is Eli." He'd never imagined ever being so close to her. The nerves in his fingers and toes tingled. He clasped his hands together to dull the sensation.

She turned toward him and raked the purple hair from her face with her hand. "What are you doing?"

He wasn't sure himself. "You're clearly upset about something. Maybe you need some company."

"I am, and I don't."

Even though she dismissed him, he couldn't bring himself to sever the tenuous connection with her and stand. "What's your name?" Something about her struck him as familiar, but he couldn't imagine what. Probably by seeing her frequently, he'd become accustomed to her.

"If you weren't Amish, I'd think you were some sort of creepy stalker." Did she have a lilt of an accent?

He placed his palm on his chest. "I mean you no harm. Won't you tell me your name?"

She changed her focus to her purple painted nails and picked at them. "Dori. Why did you sit down with me? That's not very Amish."

He gave a chuckle. "You probably won't understand this, but I felt *Gott* leading me to come over to you."

She chuffed out a breath. "God? God doesn't care about me."

"He does. Very much."

Her words rushed out. "Then why has my boyfriend kicked me out? I lost my stupid low-paying job. And I have no place to live. Trust me, God does *not* care about me."

"What about your family? You could ask them for help."

She pulled a tight smile. "Trust me, my family doesn't want anything to do with me."

"Have you asked them?"

"There's no point."

"You don't know until you try. Your family may be waiting to hear from you. Waiting for you to come home."

She shook her head. "It was nice of you to stop and try to help. You've done your good deed. You can go now."

Gut deed? Was that what she thought? If he simply needed to complete a *gut* deed, he had many neighbors he could help.

This had not been his idea. But had he done all that *Gott* had in mind for him to do?

She inclined her head toward his wagon. "Your friend is waiting for you."

"He will wait." Eli considered her. She had no job and no place to live. That likely meant she had nothing in her stomach. He stood and took a retreating step. "Come."

She glanced over her shoulder and up at him. "Why?"

He poked his thumb behind him at the sub shop. "I will buy you a sandwich."

The one visible eyebrow shifted down. "What? Really?"

"*Ja.* Come in and pick out what you want. If you don't, I'll pick for you." He reached for the door handle.

"You're serious." She scrambled to her feet.

He held the door. "Pick whatever kind of sandwich you want." With his other hand, he held up his index finger to Daniel to let him know he'd be a minute.

The male server behind the counter pulled on clear plastic gloves. "Welcome. What can I make for you?"

Rainbow Girl's voice came out small and uncertain. "I'd like the sweet onion chicken teriyaki."

"Six-inch or twelve?"

Rainbow Girl said, "Six—"

Eli spoke over her. "Twelve-inch, please."

She looked at him sideways.

He knew she had to be hungry. She could eat the other half later if she didn't want it now. She chose her bread and veggies.

He ordered two more twelve-inch sandwiches, one for himself, the other for Daniel, and got them all chips and chocolate milk. He set her food and drink on a table but didn't sit.

"I need to go now."

"Thank you. I really appreciate this." Her mouth curved up a little bit, and his insides responded happily. "I won't tell anyone you helped the strange *Englisher*—" she lifted her hands and flipped them around in tight circles "—with the colorful hair."

He should do more but didn't know what. "You should talk to your family. I'm sure they miss you."

Englisher parents had to love their children too, didn't they?

"I'm sure they don't. I've done things they'll never be able to forgive."

This poor woman had next to nothing.

"Give them a chance." He dug in his pocket and put a ten-dollar bill on the table. "Spend this on food." But there was no guarantee she would.

She stared at him.

Though he wanted to stay longer with her, he turned and hurried out before she could refuse it. He cast a glance over his shoulder. What was it he felt for this stranger? Pity? *Ja.* But there was something more to it. Compassion? *Ja.* But still more. He continued to mull it over as he approached the wagon, and the impossible truth hit him. *Attraction.*

How could that be? It certainly wasn't her appearance. It had been when she'd thanked him and smiled. It had caused his insides to wriggle like a fish trying to get away.

He couldn't deny it. She was someone he wanted to get to know better, but that would be ill-advised. The best thing to happen would be to never see her again.

Dori. Knowing her real name dispelled some of the mystery about her. He would always think of her as Rainbow Girl though.

He suspected it would be a while before he could shake her from his thoughts.

Something inside Dori ached for the handsome Amish man to stay with her a little longer. He headed out the door and toward his horse and wagon. Eli Hochstetler hadn't recognized her. Nor had the other Amish man with him. Just as well. She'd worked hard to erase any trace of her former Amish self. Eli made her long for…for… What? Something more. But what was that something? Craig? No. Then what? She stared after his retreating wagon and wanted to call him back.

How weird to see and talk to an Amish person. She hadn't done so in four years, avoiding them whenever possible.

Eli had surprised her when he bought her—an *Englisher*—a sandwich. He had always been kind even though a bit rigid and unbending with people's actions, like his father and her grandfather. The three of them would have plenty to say about all her poor choices. Choices that had been right for her at the time.

He likely had many thoughts about her hair, makeup and clothing. And what had he thought of her piercings? She chuckled to herself. If he had recognized her, no doubt he would have been horrified and wouldn't have spoken to her at all. She'd thought she'd blown it by calling herself an *Englisher*, but it seemed to have sailed right by him. She was glad he hadn't recognized her. This way she could keep this little moment she'd had with him special.

He'd looked so uncomfortable talking to her. It had been kind of cute. Eli had always been appealing. His intense brown eyes still captivated her. She'd almost told him who she was and that she knew him, but she feared it would have put him off, and she'd appreciated his kindness. He would have judged her actions as vulgar and unacceptable, but as an *Englisher*, anything she did would be viewed as merely an example of their strange ways.

Tears welled in her eyes at the thought of him being

repulsed by her if he knew. She desperately didn't want him to think poorly of her. She wanted him to like her again. What was she thinking? It must be her out of whack hormones.

With her stomach satisfied and the other half of the sandwich tucked inside her backpack, she headed down the street.

After two weeks of morning sickness and fighting with Craig, Dori had packed suitcases with her clothes, books, and various items from around the apartment, and checked herself in at a women's shelter. How pitiful her life had become.

How could Craig not want his own child?

The following morning at the shelter, she shoved her damp toothbrush into her backpack in preparation to leave for the day. Her hand hit something hard. She gripped the cold, curved metal and pulled it out. At the sight of the iron door knocker, she froze. Even though she had put it there, it surprised her. Why? Because she'd seen and talked to Eli yesterday? He'd created this in his forge. She gripped it hard. The prodigal son story came to mind.

And when he came to himself, he said, How many hired servants of my father's have bread enough and to spare, and I perish with hunger! I will arise and go to my father—

She sucked in a breath. No, she could never go back there. Would her father even let her return? He might, but her grandfather never would. Amish had a propensity for forgiveness, but her grandfather had quit speaking to her even before she'd left because of her wild ways. If he saw her now, would he even recognize her? Would any of them? Eli hadn't. She smiled at his sweetness yesterday. Thoughts of returning to the Amish people were Eli's fault. He'd put the idea in her head.

Dori shoved the iron door knocker back into her backpack.

—and will say unto him, Father, I have sinned against heaven, and before thee.

Boy, had she ever sinned.

Even shunned, as she would be if she returned, the Amish would treat her better than this. They would feed her, give her a clean bed and take care of her, even if she had to eat at a separate table from the rest of her family. Though no one would be allowed to talk to her, she would be provided for. Her child would be treated well and taken care of. Her child wouldn't go hungry if Dori was forced to remain there for an extended period, nor would it go without clothes or a bed, and it would have a roof over its head. What more did either of them need right now?

She would go back to the community until she could get a job and support herself and her child. Only a temporary solution.

And she would get to see Eli again. That thought made her insides smile.

Chapter Two

Later that morning, Dori stood in the buggy-filled yard of her parents' Amish home.

The shelter manager had told Dori that being homeless was no life for her child. She even specifically said that the Amish community would be a good place for both her and her baby.

Dori doubted that. It was strict and overshadowed by so many rules. Too many to keep track of.

She wanted to run after the car that had dropped her off but instead stood in the midst of the buggies for several minutes, contemplating what to do. The vehicles mocked her, reminding her that she didn't belong. But somewhere beyond them, inside the house, sat Eli Hochstetler. Had she not run into him and seen the potential for the Amish to treat her with even a small amount of compassion, she doubted she would have come.

She stepped between the buggies, and her breathing came in catches. She didn't want to go inside and have everyone stare at her. She'd hoped to arrive unnoticed. Just her family would know she had come. Not only would they be surprised but shocked. She couldn't turn back now. No way did she want to return to the unpredictable women's homeless shelter. The one thing she could say about the *Ordnung* rules, they made life here predictable.

She ventured toward the house she'd grown up in and climbed the porch. Sweat broke out on her upper lip. *Just look for Eli. He will welcome me.* She was sure of it.

Voices rose in a cappella with the words from hymn 131, *"Das Loblied,"* "Hymn of Praise." Always the second song.

The words floated back to her like a gentle breeze, and she mouthed the all-too-familiar hymn as she stowed her suitcases at the end of the porch. As though being drawn forward by something outside herself, she moved toward the open doorway. With a deep breath, she slipped inside at the back of the room. Fortunately, everyone was on their feet for singing. Wouldn't Eli be surprised to see her?

And there he stood in the last row on the far side in the corner. His usual place. He looked in her direction and stared for a moment with wide eyes, probably wondering why she—an *Englisher*—had invaded an Amish service. He motioned her over and pointed to his place.

Her stomach twisted even more. She shook her head, undeserving to take his seat and preferring to stand by the door for a quick exit if she needed it.

He crossed to her, causing several of the single men who always inhabited the back of the room to turn. He guided her to the bench.

She wanted to refuse, but more than that she didn't want to draw attention to herself. No going unnoticed now. She stood where he'd been, and he positioned himself between the end of the bench and the wall. "Thanks," she whispered and turned from him. She had been right about him welcoming her. At least until he found out who she was.

The man she stood next to jerked his attention forward. He'd obviously been staring. Was he the same one with Eli yesterday? She knew him but couldn't pull his name out of her tumultuous brain. It would come to her later. Rather than singing, she hummed along with the other voices, not wanting to give away her heritage. People would know all too soon who had invaded their midst.

After the next hymn ended, everyone sat. She did so as well, now grateful for a seat. She would blend in better sitting as opposed to standing by the door. As much as she could blend in with brightly colored hair and *Englisher* clothes.

How unorthodox for a woman to be among the young, unmarried men. This would cause a stir. Without enough room on the bench, Eli stood against the wall, as did a few other young men. Having him near gave her courage. Several of the men along the bench glanced in her direction. She tried to feign invisibility.

The bishop stood in the front of the room, Bishop Bontrager, her grandfather. Strict. Inflexible. Judgmental.

She held her breath. Would he see her? Of course he would with her hair. How could he miss her? She might as well be wearing a flashing neon sign on her head. But would he recognize her? Would he accept her back? He and the other leaders were hard on young people who indulged too much during *Rumspringa* or left the faith altogether. Both of which she had done.

She'd never planned to return, but here she sat. She wished she'd worn a dark beanie hat to hide her hair.

He was giving one of the three sermons that would be preached by three different men this morning. Though his voice didn't have the edge to it she remembered, it still grated on her nerves, hearing his years of admonishments echoing in her head.

Please, don't have him see me. Now she wished she *had* waited on the porch. She could've listened from there just as well.

She glanced up at Eli, who was staring at her, and her heart skipped a beat. He jerked his gaze away and to the front where it should have been. Had he been trying to figure out why an *Englisher* was here? Or had he recognized her?

She turned her attention to the bishop, who spoke about the woman caught in sin.

Strange. Dori tilted her head. Was that compassion for the woman in his voice? In times past, he would pound the point home that the *woman* had been caught in sin and would focus on *her* sin and how wrong *she'd* been.

His gaze flitted over his flock but kept returning to Dori, and finally, it rested on her. His words halted momentarily. Could he have recognized her? Even with her strange hair and makeup? What would he do now? Single her out as the sinful woman she was?

His eyes softened even more, and his lips pulled up ever so slightly at the corners. He didn't take his eyes off her as he went on. He thumped his fingertips on his chest when he emphasized that the eldest among the accusers dropped his stone first and walked away.

"'Neither do *I* condemn *thee*.'" He spoke the words as though they were just for Dori.

She swore she could see a tear roll down his cheek. Had he changed in the years she'd been gone? She couldn't imagine that he had. Too much to hope for.

When he was through, he sat in one of the chairs up front off to the side reserved for the church leaders but kept his gaze on her.

She couldn't tell if he was chastising her for being the biggest sinner of them all or if he was… Dare she hope he forgave her?

It didn't matter. Even shunned here with the Amish was better than being in the shelter out there, wondering where her next meal would come from. Scared. Alone. She would actually prefer to have people not speak to her rather than face their condemnation.

When the service concluded, Dori remained seated while others filed outside to eat lunch in the late-spring sunshine. People glanced at her on their way past or pretended not to see her at all. Just as well. Dori kept her head down when her parents passed by. Everyone left except Dori, Eli Hochstetler and the bishop.

Eli motioned toward the door and spoke in English. "We eat a meal together. You're welcome to join us."

She delighted in his kindness and wanted to savor it. The fact that he was handsome didn't hurt. His nearness fortified her nerves.

Bishop Bontrager approached and spoke in *Deutsch*. "I'll see to this young lady."

Though Eli appeared reluctant, he gave a nod and left without protest.

She wanted to call back her benefactor. Her champion. The bishop held out his hands, palms up, continuing in *Deutsch*. "You've come home. At long last." He *had* recognized her. What was this welcoming attitude?

"Ja. Ne." But she *was* here, and this *had* once been her home. *"Ja."* Dori stared at his hands a moment, then put hers in his. She didn't know what else to say. Should she come right out and tell him she was going to have a baby? She should tell him, but he seemed genuinely pleased to see her. She didn't want to destroy that. Didn't want to see the disappointment on his face when he learned how far she'd fallen. She wanted to bask in the joy and love she felt at this moment. What must he think of her wild appearance?

"You've grown up in the years you've been away." He squeezed her hands. "Let's go tell your *vater* and *mutter* you've returned."

Dori pulled free. *"Ne.* Not out there. Not in front of everyone. I didn't realize it was service Sunday. I hadn't even realized it was Sunday at all."

He pulled his eyebrows down. "You didn't know it was Sunday?"

She shouldn't have admitted that. She braced herself for a lecture about going to church.

But instead, he held up a hand. "Wait here, and I'll bring them to you." He walked out, but stopped at the door and stared at her. "Welcome home, *meine enkelin*." He left.

Was she welcome? Would she be welcomed by her *vater* and *mutter*? If the bishop could welcome her, then certainly her parents would. She put one hand on her stomach. But would she still be welcomed when she told them? Even the New Order Amish here in Elkhart County, Indiana, had their limitations of what they would tolerate. She had gone far outside those boundaries.

She should leave. Before the bishop and her parents returned. But how could she escape without being seen? If she left now, where would she go? Return to the shelter? To Craig? He'd made it clear that the only way he'd have her back was if she "got rid of it" as he put it. She caressed her growing stomach. Her baby was a person to be loved and who would love her. Not something to be gotten rid of.

When the door opened, Dori jumped and spun around. She faced her parents.

Bishop Bontrager motioned toward her. "Our Dorcas has come home."

She cringed at her given name.

Mutter's face lit up, and she rushed to Dori and hugged her. "You're home. You're finally home."

Dori hugged her in return. She'd missed her. "I'm back." Sort of. No sense clouding the moment by telling them she didn't plan to stay.

Vater hung back. "Until the next time she doesn't like the *Ordnung* rules."

Two out of three people happy to see her wasn't so bad. Or was that three out of four if she counted Eli?

Would she be forced to abide by the *Ordnung* if her stay was only temporary? Would she follow the rules for the sake of her child? The *Ordnung* offered a degree of safety and security. Two things she needed most right now. "I will try." She couldn't promise anything more than that.

He gave a nod. "Then welcome home." But his words weren't filled with cheer or even pleasure, only resignation. "Come eat."

She couldn't have pretense and secrets if she was going to live under her *vater*'s roof. When he found out, it would be worse. "Wait. I have to tell you something first."

Three sets of questioning eyes stared at her.

Best to get it over with quickly. "I'm going to have a baby."

Mutter clapped her hands together and put them to her lips. "Our first grandchild."

Vater glanced around and then narrowed his eyes at her. "Where is your husband?"

The temptation to tell him that her "husband" had died tickled her tongue. He would accept that, and everything would be fine. No one would have any reason to shun her or hate her.

But she couldn't.

"I have no husband."

Mutter gasped.

Vater glared. "So this is why you have returned. Where is the *vater*?"

"He doesn't want us anymore." Craig's rejection had hurt more than anything.

"See where your sin has gotten you?"

"Andrew," Bishop Bontrager said.

Her *vater* narrowed his gaze at his own *vater*, the *bishop* of the whole community. "She has brought this on herself. I want no part of her."

Mutter gasped again. "Andrew, you can't mean that."

"I do. And you are to have nothing to do with her either."

The bishop put his hand on his son's shoulder. "We

must all forgive trespasses as the *Vater* in heaven forgives us."

Her *vater* shot his hand out to the side, pointing at the floor. "Not this. If we forgive her, what does it say to all the other young people going on *Rumspringa*?"

The bishop straightened. "That we show grace and mercy as our Heavenly *Vater* shows grace and mercy to us."

"*Ne*. It shows we condone their actions. Then every girl will return pregnant and every boy a *vater*-to-be."

"Release the rock in your hand, Andrew."

Her *vater* glared. "You might be able to forgive her, but I can't." He wheeled around and walked to the door. He stopped and turned. "Come, Leah."

Dori's *mutter* glanced between her daughter and her husband.

Dori gave *Mutter* a nod that she understood her *mutter* wasn't abandoning her like *Vater*.

Her *mutter* gave her a weak smile and followed her husband out.

Dori blinked, freeing the tears pooled in her eyes. Then she turned to the bishop. "What do I do now? I thought my parents would allow me to come back. I have no place to live, no money and no job. I assumed I'd be shunned, but I'd at least have a roof over my head."

"You have a roof."

"I don't want to be in my *vater*'s *haus* if he can't tolerate my presence."

"You'll come and live under *meine* roof. I'm across the yard in the *dawdy haus*."

This was a turnaround. She'd thought her *grossvater*, the bishop, would be the one to reject her and her *vater* to welcome her. "The *dawdy haus* isn't big enough. It has only one bedroom."

"We'll manage. I'll hear no arguing over the matter."

"Danki." She needed to know where she stood in the community. "Am I to be shunned?"

The bishop smiled. Or was that her *grossvater* smiling at her? "Did you join church before you left?"

"Ne." But he knew that already.

"Then there are no grounds on which to shun you. You don't fall under the *Ordnung* or church rules." He smiled broadly. "So we can eat together."

"Don't you eat at the big *haus* with *Vater, Mutter* and the rest of the family?"

"I did. But now that you're here, you can cook for the two of us."

"Are you sure?" It was as though he was choosing to be cut off like one who was shunned.

"Let's call it your rent for staying in *meine* home."

"Danki. I appreciate this so much, but I have to ask. Why this change of heart? You never would have accepted me home before."

"You aren't the only one who did some growing up while you were gone. I'm an old man. I don't want to spend what few years I have left at odds with *meine* family."

"But you are at odds with your son because of me."

"Andrew will come around. Given enough time."

Would she be here long enough to see his change? And when she left again, it would confirm that he'd been right about her.

Eli Hochstetler had stared in wonder when Bishop Bontrager left the *haus* and then returned with his son Andrew Bontrager and his son's wife, Leah. Why had the Bontragers gone back inside? Why would the bishop want them to meet Rainbow Girl? Unless…they knew her? But how could they? Who was she?

He thought hard and could come up with only one name. Dorcas?

Couldn't be. But the twisting in the pit of his stomach and the leap of his heart said otherwise.

Rainbow Girl *had* seemed familiar, and now he knew why. She *was* Dorcas Bontrager, the sweet girl who had turned her back on her Amish life.

And him.

Anger boiled inside him. Why hadn't she told him? Why had she returned? Was she here to stay?

Someone nudged him. "Did you invite that *Englisher* here to make a website for you?"

Eli turned to Daniel. "*Ne.* I had no idea she would show up."

"Did you tell her you needed a website? Maybe she decided to see if she could persuade you. *Englishers* can be pushy that way. Thinking they know better than we do."

"Don't talk about her like that. I told her to go to her family." Apparently, she'd taken his advice.

"I wonder why she came."

Eli held his tongue.

"Are you coming to eat?"

"Not yet. You go on."

Daniel walked away.

Soon, the door to the *haus* opened, and Andrew Bontrager stood in the threshold. Quickly, his wife joined him, and they left. Neither happy. One angry, the other on the verge of tears.

Where were the bishop and Rainbow Girl?

He longed to see her, to make sure it was indeed her—or that it wasn't. Which did he want? Both. Neither. So he stood at the bottom of the steps, anticipating. Debating. Should he go inside?

Eli startled at the appearance of the bishop and Rainbow Girl in the doorway, and he stuttered out words. "B-Bishop Bontrager."

The bishop's eyes widened. "Ah, Eli. This is *meine enkelin*, Dorcas. And this is Eli Hochstetler. But you two already know each other."

His gut twisted, and his heart leaped. He stared hard to find some glint of the Amish girl who'd once lived among them. "Dorcas?"

She spoke in *Deutsch*. "*Ja*. It's me. I'm Dori now."

Even after all this time, he'd still imagined her very Amish. Not...*this*. "Nice to see you. Again."

Dorcas smiled a smile to rattle a man's nerves. "Good to see you again too, Eli."

Eli understood. The lilt of an accent he'd heard came from her Amish roots.

The bishop stepped forward and pointed to the other end of the porch. "Eli, would you get *meine enkelin*'s suitcases and take them to the *dawdy haus*?"

He glanced down at the stoop. "She's staying?"

"*Ja. Meine enkelin* has come home."

Dorcas's expression said she wasn't pleased about it.

Bishop Bontrager gave him a pointed look. "Will you bring them?"

Eli wanted to take them for the Amish girl who had left him behind but not for the outrageous *Englisher* who had returned in her place.

"I can get my own things." Dorcas stepped in that direction.

"Of course, I'll get them." Eli bounded up the four steps in two strides. He gripped the two side handles and hoisted the suitcases.

Rainbow Girl pointed. "They have wheels."

He extended one index finger. "They'll bounce around too much going over the grass." For some strange reason, having her back in the community both excited and repelled him. How could Dorcas—the rebel—interest him? He followed Bishop Bontrager and Rainbow Girl.

As they passed the crowd dishing up food and eating, many stared at Dorcas.

Eli wanted to tell everyone to stop gawking, that they were being rude. He wanted to protect her.

Inside the *dawdy haus*, Bishop Bontrager indicated next to the door. "You can set them there."

He didn't want to be dismissed so soon. He wanted to stay with Rainbow Girl a little longer. "I can take them—"

The bishop lifted his hand. "Here will be fine."

He set down the suitcases. "Is there anything else I can do to help?" He glanced at Rainbow Girl, who was watching him.

She gave him a small smile in return that delighted him.

The bishop said, "*Ne*. That will be all. *Danki*."

Though Eli wanted to stay, he backed out the door and continued until he stumbled down the two steps. He didn't need this, any of this. He needed to stop thinking about Rainbow Girl and focus on getting his ironworks business going this summer. And he wouldn't be asking her for any help whatsoever.

He'd also planned to start courting this summer. He hadn't decided who to court yet. But it was high time he took a wife.

Dorcas returning changed everything.

Not necessarily for the *gut*.

Chapter Three

A hole widened inside Dori after Eli left. She glanced around the tiny *dawdy haus*. Her and Craig's apartment had been bigger. And she might have been able to mistake this dwelling for any apartment except for the lack of a big flat-screen TV and a laptop.

The bishop grasped the roller handle of one of the suitcases and aimed for the short hallway with three doors. "The bedroom's back here."

She gripped the side of the extended handle. "I won't take your bedroom. I'll be fine out here." Fortunately, the full-size couch looked comfortable enough. Couldn't be any worse than the shelter beds.

He stared at the couch. "But...I...I want you to feel welcome."

She patted his hand, still on her roller bag. "I do. *Danki.*" She wouldn't be staying for long and didn't want to put him out. The less comfortable she was, the better.

He released his hold on the bag.

How surreal to be here. It was as though she were walking through some bizarre dream. "I appreciate you letting me stay with you for a few days." Strange that she'd so easily slipped back into speaking *Deutsch*. Almost natural. The rest of her short stay wouldn't be so effortless.

"I can't begin to express how pleased I am you've returned."

"I haven't *returned*. I just need a place to stay until I can get things sorted out." Or until Craig came for her.

"But you're here, and I'm grateful for that."

"I'm grateful too. If you hadn't taken me in, I would've had to return to the homeless shelter."

"Homeless?" His eyes widened. "You are never homeless. You always have a place with me. Let's go get some food."

Dori's insides turned cold. "You go. I'll stay here." Though hungry, she didn't want to face the others and be stared at again. Walking from the big *haus* to the *dawdy haus* had been bad enough, like running a gauntlet or being an oddity in a freak show.

"You have to eat."

She was about to lie and say she wasn't hungry when her stomach growled loudly. Why couldn't it have waited a minute or two? "I can't. You go."

He hesitated. "Everyone will be glad for your return."

Dori shook her head. "You saw the way *Vater* reacted."

"But your *mutter* was pleased, as others will be."

"She's not allowed to be pleased." That was clear enough.

"It will be fine. You'll see."

She wasn't convinced. Chances were that more people than not would have a mind-set like her *vater*'s.

If Eli were here to go with her, she might be brave enough to risk it. "I'll pass."

After a moment, he nodded. "I'll bring you a plate of food. Make yourself at home." He scuttled out the door.

Eli ignored the smells of food and the buzz of people talking around the lunch tables in the yard. Instead, he stood, leaning against a large, blooming fruit tree that had been grafted to bear three different varieties of apples in season. Waiting. For what, he wasn't sure. To catch a glimpse of Rainbow Girl? *Ne.* Her unruly image was seared into his brain. The bishop to come out? *Ne.* He would wonder why Eli was standing around and not filling a plate. Eli had no idea why he stood here, just that he couldn't tear his gaze from the *dawdy haus* she'd disappeared into.

Daniel once again came up to him, holding a plate heaped with food this time. "Who is she? And why has she gone into the bishop's *haus*? Is she planning to convert?"

Eli doubted that. Should he tell Daniel who she was? He would find out soon enough. "She's Dorcas Bontrager, the bishop's *enkelin.*"

"Are you serious?"

Eli wished he wasn't.

"Weren't you sweet on her?"

Dorcas? *Ja.* This *Englisher*? *Ne.* "That was a long time ago. I've gotten over her." But had he? His flip-floppy emotions told him there was still something there. But what?

"You better get some food before all the *gut* stuff is gone." Daniel took a big bite of the chicken that was on his plate.

"I'll be there in a few minutes. You go on."

Though Daniel seemed reluctant, he walked off.

When the bishop exited, Eli pushed away from the trunk.

Bishop Bontrager made eye contact and headed in his direction. "Why aren't you eating?"

"Um… I didn't know if you would need any more help."

The old man's eyes brightened. "I do have something. Let's fill plates and take them back to *meine haus* and discuss what I have in mind."

Back to where *she* was. This was a change from being dismissed a few minutes ago. The bishop wanted Eli to help him? An honor.

At the table laden with food, Eli loaded a plate for himself, then carried the second plate the bishop had filled. For Rainbow Girl, no doubt. He would get to eat lunch with her. His heart skipped a beat. Maybe figure out how the Amish girl he'd known could turn into the *Englisher* one who'd returned.

Before they reached the *dawdy haus*, Andrew Bontrager, the bishop's son and Rainbow Girl's *vater*, approached. "You're feeding her in there? Is she too embarrassed to eat with everyone else?"

She did need to eat, and she couldn't exactly blend in. No Amish liked to stand out from the others. But then, she wasn't Amish. She had designed her appearance to draw attention to herself.

The bishop held up his hand. "Give her time. Our ways are a lot to get used to."

Andrew scowled. "She was raised with our ways and threw them away. She knew exactly what it would be like returning in her state." He strode away, shaking his head.

The old man sighed. "Dorcas isn't the only one who needs a little time to adjust." He opened the *dawdy haus* door and walked in.

If Rainbow Girl planned to stay for any length of time, everyone would need time to adjust. Eli followed and froze just inside. His breath caught.

Rainbow Girl lay curled up on one end of the sofa. Eyes closed. Even, slow breathing. Out of place in an Amish home. Though she gave an unreal feel to the room, his insides felt happy to see her here. He could almost see the sweet, pretty girl from his youth.

Bishop Bontrager put a finger to his lips, then pointed at the table and whispered, "Let's sit."

Eli set the two plates he held on to the table. A sound from across the room drew him around.

Rainbow Girl swung her legs off the couch and sat up.

His mouth reacted by pulling into a smile. He straightened it.

Bishop Bontrager waved her over. "I'm sorry we disturbed you, but since you're up, come eat."

"I learned to sleep light at the shelter." She padded over in stocking feet, socks that were like gloves with a different color for each individual toe. She sat in one of the chairs.

The shelter?

The bishop looked at the one remaining chair, then at Eli. "Would you go to the big *haus* and bring another chair?"

Eli shook his head. "I'll stand."

"Are you sure?"

Nodding, Eli picked up his plate and leaned against the counter. If he left, she might disappear like a mirage. Something inside him needed her to stay.

Bishop Bontrager gave a nod and sat. "I'll say a blessing for our food."

Rainbow Girl's fork, with a chunk of potato on it, hovered an inch from her open mouth. She set the utensil on her plate. After the bishop prayed, she picked up her fork once more. "I've missed really good potato salad." She put the bite into her mouth.

Eli stared at Rainbow Girl's lip. How could she eat with that piece of metal in her upper lip? His own lip twitched. The loop in the side of her nose made his itch, but he resisted the urge to scratch it.

He studied her to find some vestige of the girl she once was. What had happened to that girl he grew up with who bested him in math every time? Where had the girl gone who'd brought him a handicapped puppy? How had she turned into…this?

She didn't stop eating until her plate had nothing left. Hungry, indeed. It had been *gut* that he bought her the larger sandwich yesterday.

Eli hurriedly took bites and swallowed the barely chewed food. "Bishop, what is it you need me to do?"

"Let's finish our food first. It'll be better to show you." In other words, eat, no talking.

Eli ate without looking at *her* again so she wouldn't realize he'd been paying more attention to her than his food.

When finished, the bishop pushed his plate away from him. "Now, Eli, about that project I have in mind."

Project? That sounded big. Would it take away from Eli getting his business started?

The bishop stood and retrieved a measuring tape from a kitchen drawer. "Follow me." He walked down the short hallway to the back door opposite the front one. Hooks hung on the walls leading to the exit. A bedroom door to the right and bathroom to the left.

Eli had actually helped build this little *haus* many years ago when the bishop had turned over his farm to Andrew. Eli glanced at Rainbow Girl, who shrugged. He supposed he should follow and headed down the hall. She trailed behind.

The bishop stopped at the end of the hall and indicated the door. "I want to extend this another eight to ten feet." He opened the door and walked down the steps outside onto the grass and turned around. "Come."

The rear of the *dawdy haus* faced away from the crowd of people eating and playing.

Eli stepped aside to let Rainbow Girl exit ahead of him. She did. In stocking feet.

He followed this time. "Why do you want a longer hallway out into the yard?"

The old man smiled like a little boy. "For the extra bedroom, of course." He strode about ten feet straight out from the *haus*. "Move the door to here. I still want to get cross ventilation. No sense being impractical."

Eli's mind whirled. Building onto his *dawdy haus* seemed impractical. What could he possibly need another bedroom for? Maybe he'd heard wrong. "You… want to make…*your* bedroom bigger?" That didn't make sense either.

"*Ne*. A bedroom for Dorcas." He turned to the right and held out his hands to indicate the space.

So she planned to stay for quite some time. Or at

least, the bishop thought she would stay long enough to need a room.

Rainbow Girl stepped forward. "You can't do this. I'll be fine on the couch."

He waggled his hand at her. "Nonsense. The couch will never do."

Rainbow Girl folded her arms. "I won't let you."

"*Uf*, it's *meine haus*. I'll do with it what I like."

The bishop turned to Eli. "What do you say? Will you help me build it?"

"Why doesn't she stay at the big *haus*?" That would be the easier option, and there would be plenty of room for her.

"Because she's staying with me. Now, will you help?"

Rainbow Girl turned to Eli. "Tell him *ne*." Apparently, she didn't intend to stay.

Again, Eli wanted to say *ne* to doing something for the *Englisher* girl who had returned. Since she didn't want the room—and he really had no other choice— he sided with the bishop. "*Ja*. I'll help." Then maybe he could find the girl she once was under her facade.

"Not only one room, but a smaller one across the hall, as well." Bishop Bontrager spun around opposite the first room he'd indicated and thrust out his arms. "No sense wasting this space."

"For what?"

The bishop waved his hand in the air. "No need to get into all that right now. I'd like to go into town tomorrow and purchase the lumber."

This definitely meant Eli would need to put off making progress on his business. "What about your son? Won't he help you?"

"Andrew is being stubborn."

Rainbow Girl planted her hands on her hips. "Would you drop this? He won't agree."

Eli didn't know if she was referring to him or her *vater*. It didn't really matter. He *had* agreed, and the bishop could overrule his son, so, the addition would be built. "I can use *meine vater*'s wagon. What time shall I pick you up?"

Rainbow Girl rolled her eyes. "Don't waste your time."

The bishop turned to his *enkelin*. "It won't be a waste." He swung his gaze to Eli. "I'll check with Andrew and see if he'll allow us to use his wagon without a fuss. It'll be more convenient."

"Seriously?" Rainbow Girl threw her hands up and headed toward the doorway. "Men think they always know what's best." She disappeared inside, still muttering.

Eli frowned. But men did. Even with all that makeup, he could remember how cute she was when she got mad.

Bishop Bontrager clasped him on the shoulder. "Don't worry about her. She'll see the value of it in time."

A part of Eli found a little pleasure in her being upset with him. She had rejected the community and her family, so she had no say in matters. Another part longed to mend this breach. It rankled to have her angry with him when he'd done nothing wrong, but it shouldn't, and that rankled even more.

The bishop held out the tip of the measuring tape. "Take it down to that corner of the *haus* so we can figure out how much lumber to purchase."

Eli wasn't sure this was a *gut* idea, but he was the bishop, so Eli did as instructed.

Andrew Bontrager came around the corner. "What are you doing, *Vater*?"

"Eli is going to help me build another bedroom onto the *haus*."

"What do you need a second bedroom for?"

"I think you know."

Andrew pointed toward the *dawdy haus*'s back doorway. "For her?"

"Ja."

Eli glanced toward the *haus*. Rainbow Girl stood there with her arms crossed. He hadn't seen her return to the opening.

"Why bother? She'll only leave again. Then all the time and materials and work will be for nothing."

So Andrew didn't believe she would stay. Did he want her to leave? Did Eli? *Ne.* He definitely wanted her to stay. Didn't he?

The bishop held his hands out to his sides. "*'We should...be glad; for this thy brother—'* or sister in this case *'—was dead, and is alive again; and was lost, and is found.'* Where is your forgiveness?"

"Forgiveness is for the repentant. Something *she* is not." Andrew spun around and strode away.

Bishop Bontrager gazed toward his *enkelin*. "He'll come around, Dorcas."

"Why's that? Because he *didn't* inherit your stubborn streak?" She disappeared inside.

Chapter Four

The following morning, Dori had slept late—well, late for an Amish. She threw back the blanket and sat up on the couch.

It took some doing, but she'd managed to convince the bishop to stay in his room and let her sleep in the living room. She'd slept more soundly than she had in over a month since being kicked out of Craig's apartment. She had no more worries that anyone would steal her belongings during the night. Sleeping in sweatpants and a T-shirt rather than her jeans and jacket had helped, as well.

The bishop didn't appear to be anywhere in the *haus*. Had he already left with Eli? She pictured Eli's kind face when he'd bought her a sandwich two days ago. Had she missed seeing him this morning?

She heard a sound on the porch, as though something or someone had stepped on a creaky board. With her hand, she pushed aside the blue curtain enough to see out.

Her *mutter* hurried away from the *dawdy haus* across the lawn back to the big *haus*.

What had she been doing here? Had she intended to come for a visit, then changed her mind? *Ne.* She wouldn't defy *Vater.* Then why?

Out of curiosity, Dori opened the front door. On the porch sat a bundle of neatly folded fabrics. She picked up the pile and shut the door.

She spread out the clothes on the couch. *Mutter* had delivered two cape dresses—one royal blue, the other a medium pink—two aprons—one white and one black—and a white *kapp.* In the *kapp* lay several bobby pins. Everything Dori needed to dress the part of an Amish woman. These looked suspiciously like the garments she'd left behind. *Mutter* was welcoming her home even if *Vater* wasn't. *She* wanted Dori to fit in. To look Amish. To stay.

But Dori didn't want any of those things. She had been away for several years and had returned in shame. If she hadn't gotten pregnant and Craig hadn't thrown her out, she would never have come back. Being destitute and desperate had forced her home.

Home?

Was this home? For the time being, because she had no other option. If only Craig would have accepted their baby. No matter how much she needed her Amish family, this would never be home again.

She fingered the pink dress. *Mutter* remembered it had been her favorite color as a girl.

Dori wouldn't feel right wearing Amish clothes. That would give everyone the impression she had come home to stay. Which she hadn't. She was no more Amish than Craig. Or any *Englisher.* She hadn't fitted in before she left and didn't fit in now. Her *vater* and the bishop had repeatedly chastised her for one thing or another, trying to make her into a *gut* Amish woman, but she never could do things quite right, questioned too many of the rules. She'd been a disappointment to everyone. It had been best to leave. For everyone.

Though unwilling to return and no longer Amish, she did need help right now.

She hadn't expected to have a warm welcome, but she hadn't expected *Vater* to scorn her as he had. And she certainly hadn't expected the bishop, of all people, to take her in. Of anyone, she would have expected him to be the toughest on her, but he was the most welcoming. What had caused his attitude change? If he could show her mercy and grace, maybe there was hope that her *vater* would soften toward her, as well. Would Eli too? She hoped so.

She took the pile of Amish clothes and tucked them behind the couch's end table in the corner. She didn't need the bishop pestering her to wear them.

After taking a *gut* long shower, she frowned at her brown roots in the mirror. She wouldn't be touching those up anytime soon.

Overnight, her stomach seemed to have swelled so much that her jeans were no longer big enough to close. She settled for her lime-green sweatpants and an oversize neon orange T-shirt. Definitely not authorized Amish colors, but they fitted over her growing middle.

Now, for breakfast.

A single rinsed bowl with a spoon sat in the bottom of the kitchen sink. It looked as though the bishop had had cold cereal for breakfast. Or had he gone to the big *haus*?

No matter. She opened cupboards and drawers until

she had a spoon, bowl and two boxes of cereal. The first, bran flakes with raisins, and the second, sugar-coated corn flakes. His version of sweetening his cereal. She was glad to see he hadn't changed in that respect. She mixed the two in her bowl and poured the milk. She'd actually missed this.

When she was a very little girl, from about age six until she was ten or so, she would sneak across the yard to the *dawdy haus* and eat breakfast with him on Saturday mornings. She laughed to herself. She'd thought no one knew, that it was her and *Grossvater*'s secret, but *Mutter* likely watched her skip across the grass, then pretended to be worried over her absence.

Then things began to change. Kathleen Yoder had defied the church leaders and the bishop by leaving the community and attending college. *Grossvater* had spoken against her actions. He'd pointed a finger in Dori's face and told her to never do anything like that. His anger had scared her, and she stopped her weekly breakfast treks to sit at his table.

Enough of thinking of things lost. She needed to wash her clothes so she could wear something else tomorrow.

Sometime later, noise from behind the *dawdy haus* drew her to the door. She opened it.

In the grass stood a wagon full of lumber as well as three young Amish men with the bishop. One was Eli. She allowed herself a moment to savor Eli's presence, then studied the other two. Who were they? Daniel Burkholder, and the other was…Benjamin Yoder. So the bishop had used his influence to rope in more help. How many more would show up at his request?

Eli hoisted several two-by-fours at once that had to be ten feet long. Smithing had made him quite strong. The other two young men worked together to carry an equal stack. While the bishop carried smaller items like a bag of nails, hand tools and other lightweight things. Eli set his load in the grass and headed back to the wagon for more. His gaze fell on her, and she smiled. He froze. His eyes widened, as though he'd been caught raiding the kitchen in the middle of the night.

She glanced down at herself. She must look a fright in her brightly colored sweatpants and top…and no makeup. Or had the bishop told him about her condition? She hoped not. She didn't want the tenuous bond between them to be broken. She resisted the urge to place her hands on her rounding belly and leaned a little forward so her baggy T-shirt would camouflage it better. He'd been careful not to mention that the smaller room would be for the baby. She appreciated that. She wasn't ashamed of being pregnant, but for some reason, she didn't want Eli to know. Maybe she would be gone before he ever found out.

This was foolishness. "Don't you need a building permit before you start?" Dori had hoped the bishop would have to wait a couple of weeks before one was issued, giving her a chance to make other arrangements.

The bishop waved a piece of paper in the air. "Got one. Since this is a simple addition with no plumbing, they have a swift process to grant us permits without delay."

Some Amish obtained waivers to exclude parts of construction that went against their community's *Ordnung* but were mandatory in *Englisher* homes, like indoor plumbing, smoke and carbon monoxide detectors.

This wasn't new construction, merely a simple addition. But this New Order Amish community had most of the same conveniences as people in the outside world, so there wasn't usually a need to get a waiver, which would take time.

Now, she was going to feel guilty when she left because he'd put in all this money, time, effort and supplies for this project. Probably his plan. A way to shame her into staying. She doubted he could be stopped if he didn't want to be. His son had probably tried. Maybe she could talk to Eli and convince him to delay the work.

Doubtful. She'd seen his resolve solidify when she'd tried to get him to turn the bishop down for this project. He apparently planned to be as stubborn as the bishop. The image of Craig popped into her mind. He was stubborn too. She pushed thoughts of him aside for the time being.

For now, she turned her attention back to the activity outside. She would like to plant herself on the stoop and watch Eli while he worked, but that would make everyone feel awkward.

So she stayed for a minute before closing the door and taking the impressive image of the blacksmith with her.

With Eli fresh on her mind, Dori headed back to the living room. On her way, she checked on the clothes she'd left to dry in the bathroom. They hung over the shower rod and dripped into the tub as well as onto a towel on the floor. They should be fully dry by morning. She would've hung her *Englisher* clothes outside, but that would have drawn unwanted attention to her family. She needed to remain as invisible as possible during her stay.

She opened her backpack on the couch and retrieved her laptop and cell phone as well as their chargers. Then she unplugged the coffee maker and toaster, and plugged in her devices, stringing the cords over to the table. The phone cord didn't reach, so she slid the table closer to the counter.

The bishop probably never imagined having such electronics in his *haus*. But maybe he should. More and more Amish were forced to have websites for on-line businesses. With farmland becoming increasingly more scarce to purchase, many had to resort to working for various manufacturers or home-building companies, or starting their own construction business or other ventures. The ones with businesses needed websites to draw customers from outside the community. *Englishers* were nuts for anything Amish made. Foolish people.

She opened her laptop and powered it up. Fortunately, Janis at the shelter, who stole other people's property, never discovered Dori had this. While she waited for her laptop, she switched on her cell phone and turned it into a hot spot to get Wi-Fi. The service would likely be glitchy, but she had unlimited data, and it would be better than nothing. How had she grown up without computers and the internet?

She logged on to her email account. All junk mail. Nothing from Craig. Working to the sound of clunking lumber being stacked and male voices, she turned her efforts to searching for a job. After an hour of filling out online applications, she made herself toast with peanut butter and returned to the table. Needing a break from job hunting, she opened a new browser window and let her fingers hover over the keys. What should she search for?

For fun, she typed in *Eli Hochstetler* and hit Enter. To her surprise, hundreds of posts came up from various social media platforms. After the first page of results, the rest were obviously not relevant. She found three that seemed like they were referring to *her* Eli. All three raved about his ironwork. She clicked on each one and read. One for an herb chopper, the second for a kitchen knife and the third for a weather vane. Pictures for all three items, but none of Eli directly. His muscled arm wielding a hammer in one, the back of his head in another, his rugged profile in the third. She lingered on that picture the longest. Why were Amish so set against having their picture taken? It was only a picture. And Eli photographed well.

Then she studied the backgrounds of all three pictures. Multiples of similar items like the ones in the posts. It appeared as though Eli Hochstetler had gone into business, making more than just horseshoes. *Gut* for him. He'd always loved pounding on iron. She'd often wondered if he liked it because that was an acceptable way of letting out his aggression. But he never acted angry, like he needed to find a way to disguise the emotion. He genuinely seemed as though he simply enjoyed smithing.

She dug in her backpack and pulled out the door knocker. He had always done *gut* work. He must have a website. She would like to see all the things he'd made. After trying every variation of website names she could think of for him, her efforts yielded nothing. How disappointing.

* * *

Eli glanced at the *dawdy haus* again, but since that first glimpse, Rainbow Girl hadn't shown herself. What was she doing inside?

Bishop Bontrager took hold of the horse's harness. "I'm going to go unhitch Nelly and turn her out in the field."

Eli raised up from where he set a bag of powdered cement. "I can do that if you want me to."

"*Danki*, but I can do it." The bishop walked the big draft horse away, pulling the wagon.

Eli turned to the other two and grasped the handle of one of the shovels. "Let's dig a shallow trench for the cinder blocks first." They would form the foundation of the addition. The string lines had already been set out.

Benjamin Yoder took the other shovel.

Daniel Burkholder grabbed the pick. "I can't believe the bishop is letting an outrageous *Englisher* live in his home. And building her a room."

Eli could hardly believe it himself, but that was *not* something to voice out loud. One didn't question the bishop. Besides, the bishop's actions fell under their Amish rules of forgiveness. "Why shouldn't he? She's his *enkelin*."

"She abandoned our faith and is *English* now."

Though Benjamin Yoder didn't say anything, he nodded his agreement with Daniel.

Eli didn't like anyone speaking poorly of her. "She's obviously decided to return." At least he hoped that was what she'd decided.

"Dressed like that? And what about her hair? The bishop can't allow that. Do you think he's okay? He is pretty old."

"Of course, he's fine." But Eli had to wonder about the bishop, as well. In times past, he wouldn't have tolerated her appearance, but now, he seemed fine with her returning as she was. He leaned his shovel against the outside of the *haus*. "I'm going to get a drink of water. Start without me." He charged up the back steps and through the doorway, wiping his dusty boots as he entered. Then he stopped short. He shouldn't barge into a *haus* unannounced with a woman inside. *"Hallo?"*

Rainbow Girl stepped into his field of vision from the kitchen area. *"Hallo."*

His insides did funny things at the sight of her.

"Did you need something?"

He cleared his throat. "I came for a drink of water."

"Come on in." She pulled a glass out of the cupboard, filled it at the sink and handed it to him.

"Danki."

She gifted him with a smile. *"Bitte.* How's it going out there?"

He smiled back. "Fine." He gulped half the glass, then slowed down to sips. No sense rushing.

After a minute, she folded her arms. "Go ahead. Ask your question."

"What?"

"You obviously want to ask me something. What is it? Why do I color my hair all different colors? Why do I dress like this? Why did I leave? What is it?"

She posed all *gut* questions, but not the one he needed an answer to. A question that was no business of his to ask.

"Go ahead. Ask. I don't mind." Very un-Amish, but she'd offered. *Ne,* insisted.

He cleared his throat. "Are you going to stay?"

She stared for a moment, then looked away. Obviously, not the question she'd expected, nor one she wanted to answer.

He'd made her uncomfortable. He never should have asked. What if she said *ne*? Did he want her to say *ja*? "You don't have to tell me." He didn't want to know anymore.

She pinned him with her steady brown gaze. "I don't know. I don't want to, but I'm sort of in a bind at the moment."

Maybe for the reason she'd been so sad the other day, which had made him feel sympathy for her.

He appreciated her honesty. "Then why does our bishop think you are?"

"He's hoping I do."

His heart tightened. "Why are you giving him false hope?" Why was she giving Eli false hope?

"I'm not. I've told him this is temporary. He won't listen. Maybe you could convince him to stop this foolishness—" she waved her hand toward where the building activity was going on "—before it's too late."

He chuckled. "You don't tell the bishop what to do. *He* tells *you*."

He really should head back outside to help the others. Instead, he filled his glass again and leaned against the counter. He studied her over the rim of his glass. Did he want Rainbow Girl to stay? She'd certainly turned things upside down around here. Turned him upside down. Instead of working in his forge— where he most enjoyed spending time—he was here, and gladly so. He preferred working with iron rather than wood, but today, carpentry strangely held more appeal.

Time to get back to work. He guzzled the rest of his water and set the glass in the sink. *"Danki."* As he turned to leave, something on the table caught his attention. The door knocker he'd made years ago for Dorcas—Rainbow Girl—*ne*, Dorcas, but now Rainbow Girl had it. They were the same person, but not the same. He crossed to the table and picked up his handiwork. "You kept this?"

She came up next to him. *"Ja.* I liked having a reminder of..."

"Of what?" Dare he hope him?

She stared at him. "Of...my life growing up here."

That was probably a better answer. He didn't need to be thinking of her as anything more than a lost *Englisher.*

She pointed to her computer on the table. "I found posts online about a few of your iron pieces you made that *Englishers* bought. They all praised your work."

"I don't care about such things."

"You should. You could sell a lot more of your pieces with reviews like that, but I couldn't find your website."

"I don't have one." He'd hoped to be able to sell enough to make a living off his work. So far, he hadn't and realized he would need a website, but he didn't want to be beholden to her to get it. He wanted to be self-sufficient.

He needed to create more pieces, and now was a perfect time—with the lighter workload with *Vater's* fields rented out.

Since his *vater's* heart attack last summer, nine months ago, Eli had been entrusted with more responsibilities around the farm. Fortunately, his *vater* had decided to rent out the fields this year on the recommendation of the community's new doctor, Dr. Kathleen.

Eli could have handled running the farm himself with his younger brothers. It wouldn't have been too much for him to manage, but *Vater* thought otherwise, scared after nearly dying.

Though Eli didn't like witnessing *Vater*'s vulnerability, he secretly delighted in the lighter workload. This would give him an opportunity to design more original ironwork pieces in his blacksmith shop behind the barn. He'd consigned a few items in town but hoped to have enough creations to start his own business. Farming was *gut* and honorable work, but he liked making things with his hands, with hot metal and a hammer. He had ideas for new pieces he wanted to create.

If he could figure out how, this was his chance to get his business going. He knew it would take all the time he'd been afforded in lieu of planting and harvesting. He would need to learn all about selling on the internet, creating a website and proving to the church leaders—his *vater* being one of them—that his was a viable business worthy of internet access and use. He wouldn't have another opportunity like this. If he didn't make a go of this by the fall, he would need to give up his dream.

Rainbow Girl broke into his thoughts. "You need to have a website. You could sell a lot more of your work. *Englishers* love buying Amish-made stuff. A website can do that for you."

Ja, he knew he needed a website in order to make money from the *Englishers*. "I plan to hire an *Englisher* to do that for me." So much to do and learn to get started. A bit overwhelming.

"I can do it."

"*Ne.* I'll hire someone." He couldn't be beholden to her.

"That would be a waste of money. There are so many programs out there to help you build a site. And they're easy to use."

He could make his own site? *Ne.* "It would be better if I don't fiddle in *Englisher* things and let an *Englisher* do them."

"So you're going to pay an *Englisher* to monitor your website after it's built and tell you when you have orders? You aren't going to make any money that way. You need to monitor your own site. I can build you a site and teach you how to maintain it."

"*Ne.* I'll hire an *Englisher.*" An *Englisher* who wasn't *her.*

"But you can do this. You'll pick it up fast. I know you will. You always were the smartest boy in class. If I could learn how to do it, then you can."

She thought he was smart? He liked that. He wanted her to help him, but that wouldn't be wise. He couldn't let her do work for him. She wasn't staying. Or at least she didn't know if she was staying. How could she not know? She simply needed to make a choice. The right choice. He wouldn't let her get under his skin to just have her leave again. "*Ne.* I need to get back to work." He headed for the back door.

"Eli, wait."

He turned and resisted the urge to cross over to her. To stand next to her. To stare at her.

She dug a ten-dollar bill from her backpack. "Here. I never had a chance to buy any food with this." She held it out to him.

He waved it away. "Keep it." He strode out the door. She probably needed it more than he did.

Once in the yard again, he picked up the shovel and jabbed it into the ground. The trench would stabilize the concrete blocks of the foundation. But what would stabilize him?

He wished he'd grabbed the pick. Swinging it would have been similar to the rhythm of swinging his hammer in his forge. An action that helped him think. An action that could replace thoughts of Rainbow Girl. Instead, he was stuck with her image drifting in the front of his mind.

Chapter Five

Midafternoon, Dori sat in the shade of the front porch of the *dawdy haus*. Just about time for her younger siblings to return from school. Which ones were still school-age? John, the youngest at age ten, for sure attended school. Luke and Mark at eleven and thirteen would, as well. Sixteen-year-old Matthew had likely gone off to work with *Vater*. Nearly a man. Ruth, the second oldest, was eighteen now. Where had she spent her day? Inside the big *haus*, having been told not to talk to Dori? And the oldest at twenty-two, Dori was the biggest disappointment to her family.

An open buggy drove into the yard with Ruth at the reins. Mark sat next to her, with Luke and John in the rear seat, jostling each other.

Ruth glanced Dori's way as she drove to the barn and parked. "You boys take care of the buggy and horse. And no dillydallying." She climbed down and crossed the yard to the *dawdy haus*.

Dori squirmed in her chair. She wished she hadn't sat out in the open.

Ruth stopped at the bottom of the two steps. "Dorcas? Is that really you?"

"*Ja.* I go by Dori now." She didn't know what else to say, so she gave her sister a tight smile.

"Dori." Ruth's mouth curved up in a big grin. She set her tote bag on the steps as she climbed them. "You're home."

Dori automatically stood.

Though a bit hesitant, her sister hugged her. "I'm so happy you've returned. I've missed having *meine* sister around."

"I haven't exactly returned. This is only temporary."

"Then why is *Grossvater* building you a room?"

How many times would she have to tell people the room was the bishop's idea? "You know how he can be when he sets his mind to something. I told him I'm here only temporarily."

"Please stay. Do you know what it's like living in a *haus* with all boys? *Mutter* and I are overrun with them."

Dori understood. The *haus* had been pretty boisterous before she left. She had enjoyed time in the kitchen with her *mutter* and sister. "I don't fit in here. And I don't think *Vater* would approve of you talking to me."

"What is he going to do? Shun me? Let him. I've prayed for you to return. *Mutter* wants to come talk to you, but *Vater* forbade her."

"Didn't he forbid you, as well?"

Ruth shrugged. "Not in so many words. He said you were an *Englisher* now, and talking to *Englishers* was not a *gut* idea. Then glared at each one of us. I took his warning as a suggestion."

Oh, dear. Was her sister as defiant as Dori had been? She hoped not.

Had *Vater* told Ruth and the others about the baby? "What did *Vater* tell you about me being here?"

"That you came home because you had no place else to go, and…"

"And what?"

"He doesn't think you're going to stay. He thinks you're too *English* now. But I don't."

Dori couldn't help but to laugh. "You don't think I'm too *English*? Have you looked at me?" She held her hands out to the sides.

"All this on the outside isn't you. It's what's in your heart. And I know in mine that you are still Amish in yours."

Her sweet sister deserved the truth, even if it meant she too would reject Dori. "Ruth, the reason I've come—and it *is* just temporary—is because my boyfriend kicked me out of our apartment."

"How mean. It's *gut* you're not with him anymore."

"That's not all. He kicked me out because…because I'm pregnant. That's why *Vater* won't talk to me."

Ruth's eyes widened. "Oh."

"Craig doesn't want the baby, but I won't get rid of it." Dori caressed her lower abdomen.

A smile slowly took over Ruth's face. "I'm going to be a *tante*."

That was what her sister got out of this? No condemnation? "Don't tell anyone."

"I won't. Does *Grossvater* know?"

"*Ja.* I think that's why he's so set on building rooms for me and the baby in the *dawdy haus*. I wish he wouldn't."

Ruth took hold of one of Dori's hands. "Don't leave. You can't let your baby—*meine* little nephew or niece—grow up in a place where people discard what they don't want. You're staying, that's all there is to it." As stubborn as the bishop, and as willful as her.

Time to change the topic. "Did you pick the boys up after school?"

"*Ne.* I'm the teacher. If they don't behave, I make them walk home."

"I'm happy for you." Her sister was probably a very *gut* teacher. "You always did like school and teaching the farm animals. You would go into the chicken enclosure with your schoolbooks and try to make them learn their letters and numbers."

With an impish smile, Ruth tilted her head. "Even animals could do with a little education."

"You almost had me believing they could count."

"I still say that Claudia Clucker could count." She laughed.

Dori joined her. It felt so *gut* to laugh. How long had it been? Leave it to Ruth to make her forget her troubles if only for a brief moment.

Mark, Luke and John came out of the barn and ran over to the *dawdy haus*. They stopped short of climbing the steps and eyed Dori. Mark spoke for his younger brothers. "Can we go see how the construction is going and help out until supper?"

"Check to see if *Mutter* needs anything first."

The trio ran for the big *haus*.

Dori shook her head. "I can't believe how grown-up you are."

Ruth lifted one shoulder, then gave a mischievous

smile. "Who does *Grossvater* have working on the addition besides Eli Hochstetler?"

"Benjamin Yoder and Daniel Burkholder."

Ruth's eyes widened and gleamed. "I'll have to go see how they're doing." She pranced off the porch.

Dori caught up to her. "Is there something going on between you and Daniel?"

"Me? Why would you say that?"

"Because you lit up at the mention of his name."

Ruth stopped at the side of the *haus*. "There's nothing between me and Daniel."

"But…?"

Ruth bit her bottom lip. "I wouldn't mind if there was. But you can't tell anyone."

"My lips are sealed." Dori enjoyed chatting with her sister. She'd missed moments like this. She hooked her arm with Ruth's. "Let's go see how the men are doing."

In the backyard, all four men wielded hammers, putting the last boards on the wall-stud frames that lay in the grass, ready to be raised into place when the time came. Each one lay on the ground on the side of the wall trench where it would be put up. They'd already dug the trench and poured the footing concrete in the bottom of it.

Ruth spoke up. "*Grossvater*, you'll have three more eager workers here in a minute."

All four hammers stilled, and four heads turned. Daniel's mouth cocked up a tad on one side. Ruth's interest in the young man wasn't one-sided, it seemed.

The bishop put a hand on his lumbar region and straightened. "*Gut*. They can help us lay out the boards for the roof trusses."

Dori had a hard time thinking of the bishop as her

grossvater. He'd seemed very much the bishop before she left. But now he did seem more like a *grossvater*, like *her grossvater.* She turned her attention to Eli, who was focused on her. Her insides wiggled, and it wasn't the baby. She resisted the smile that was tickling her mouth.

The three younger boys ran up, clamoring to help.

The bishop put them to work.

Dori leaned closer to her sister and spoke softly. "So why Daniel and not Benjamin? He's closer to your age."

"Benjamin is nice enough, but he's…he's just not…"

"Daniel?"

Ruth's smile stretched. *"Ja."*

"Well, from the look Daniel gave you, I'd say the interest is mutual."

"You think so?"

"Ja." So what did that say for Eli? And for that matter, herself?

Mutter appeared from around the corner. "I've brought cookies." Her gaze sought out Dori and rested on her.

Dori stared back. She'd missed *Mutter.* She wished she could go up to her and get a hug. She wished she could sit with her on the porch. She wished *Mutter* could tell her what it was like to have a baby and give her advice on how to be a *gut mutter.*

The men and boys grabbed cookies. When the plate was nearly empty, *Mutter* crossed to Dori and Ruth. Three oatmeal-raisin cookies remained. Ruth took one. *Mutter* held the plate out to her eldest daughter.

Dori took a cookie. *"Danki."*

Mutter took the last cookie with a smile and faced

the men. "It is *gut* to have *meine* children together." She stood between her daughters.

Dori knew that *Mutter* was including her, and she welcomed the inclusion. She'd felt like an outsider with Craig ever since she told him she was pregnant two months ago. Truth be told, she'd always felt as though she didn't quite belong in the *English* world, a world she hadn't been raised in. References to TV shows and movies that everyone seemed to have seen. She'd tried to catch up, but there was so much. Some of the shows were so ridiculous, she'd given up. She feared Craig would grow tired of her not quite fitting in and send her away, so she changed her appearance as much as possible to prove to him and others she wasn't Amish.

And prove to herself.

But Craig had sent her away anyway. And she'd ended up at the shelter, where fear ruled her thoughts. But here, she didn't fear for herself or her belongings. Being here served as a sort of comfort that she didn't like. This was not the place for her, so she shouldn't find comfort here.

And yet...

Eli ate his second cookie slowly, not anxious to get back to work. He couldn't seem to take his eyes off Rainbow Girl. Was it any wonder with her brightly colored clothes and hair? Her appearance was designed to attract attention and make people stare. He was no exception, but it was more than her appearance that held him captive.

When she smiled, his insides tumbled about.

He wouldn't mind doing all this work on the *dawdy haus* if she were staying. That would give him hope.

But would she even still be here by the time they completed this project in a week or two? Would all this be for nothing?

Andrew Bontrager and Matthew, his eldest son, arrived home and came around to the rear of the *dawdy haus*, surveying the activity. Andrew shook his head. Matthew glared at his oldest sister and walked away.

Rainbow Girl's *vater* inclined his head toward his wife.

Leah Bontrager didn't turn toward her eldest daughter, but when her lips moved with her whispered words, Eli guessed they were for Rainbow Girl because she nodded. Leah strode around the work area to her husband.

Andrew waved his arm toward Ruth. "Come on, Ruth. Leave the men to their work."

Ruth stepped sideways and hooked her arm with her sister's. "I'll stay out of the way."

Open defiance? What would Andrew do?

Rainbow Girl patted her sister's arm. "Go. I don't want you in trouble with him too."

"Don't worry. *Vater* is all bluster."

Eli was grateful he stood on the side of the construction closest to the girls so he could hear their conversation. How nice of Rainbow Girl to try to protect her sister.

Andrew huffed away with Leah at his side. He allowed his three youngest boys to continue working.

The two remaining ladies sat on the back stoop, chattering. Rainbow Girl seemed happy. He liked seeing her happy. Now, instead of wondering what she was doing, he could glance her way.

Later, when as much work as possible had been

completed until the footing concrete dried in the trench, Eli went over to Rainbow Girl. He motioned toward the ragtag bits of construction. "What do you think so far? I know it doesn't look like much now, but in a day or two it'll start resembling a building."

"You know what I think."

Ja, he did. "That you're not staying." He folded his arms. "Well, I think you're wrong." Hoped she was wrong.

Ruth piped up. "I agree with you. She's staying. She just has to."

He liked the way Ruth thought. Between the bishop, Ruth and Rainbow Girl's *mutter*, she wouldn't be able to leave so easily.

With her mouth stretched wide, Ruth rose to her feet. "*Hallo*, Daniel."

His friend gave a nod. "Ruth." After staring for a moment, he turned to Eli. "Benjamin has your horse hitched to your trap." His gaze returned to Ruth.

Eli nodded. "We should go. I'll come back tomorrow to lay the concrete blocks for the foundation."

Rainbow Girl squinted up at him. The sun on her face made her appear to be glowing. "What about your forge? You don't want to neglect your work there."

"If I'm needed, *meine* family knows where to find me, and I'll do some work this evening after supper."

"You work too hard. You should rest. Take tomorrow off."

He knew what she was doing. She was trying to delay progress on the addition. She wouldn't succeed.

He touched the brim of his straw hat. "I'll see you in the morning." He turned and left. He would see her again in about thirteen hours. He mentally shook his head. It wasn't right for him to be thinking about when he would see Rainbow Girl again. He should think of other things. Like what to make this evening in his forge. Perhaps an herb chopper with a rainbow-arch handle. Or a cooking spoon with a rainbow. Would she like a candleholder?

There he went again, letting his thoughts get tangled up around her. He needed to do something drastic to clear her from his head.

After he'd dropped off Daniel and Benjamin at their respective houses, he pulled his two-wheeled trap into the Rosenbergs' yard. Mary was as *gut* as any girl to court. He parked and knocked on the door.

Saul Rosenberg, Mary's *vater*, opened the door. "Eli? What are you doing here? It's almost suppertime."

"I know. I'm on *meine* way home. May I speak to you a moment?" Eli took a step in retreat to indicate he wished to speak privately. No sense in the whole family knowing his business.

"Ja." Saul came out onto the porch.

As he did so, Eli could see Mary in the kitchen with her *mutter*. She glanced up at him from setting the table, and smiled. He smiled back. Mary was a *gut* choice.

Saul closed the door. "What is it?"

"Your daughter Mary. I was thinking…to ask to… maybe court her."

Saul smiled. *"Thinking* to ask? *Maybe?* But you aren't sure?"

Eli didn't reply. He couldn't, because he wasn't sure. "I…"

"Let me save you some trouble. Mary already has an

offer to be courted. I'm not sure she's as excited about it as the boy is, but she did say *ja*."

Unexpected relief swept through Eli.

"If the courtship is broken, I'll let you know."

"Danki." Eli bounded off the porch, into his trap and quickly set Dutch into motion. He shouldn't be this pleased with being turned down. He thought of Rainbow Girl. She didn't need to know about this. Irritation displaced his happiness. He shouldn't be thinking so much of her. Every time he turned around, she dallied in his thoughts. Why did she have to return? Because she was raised here, and this was where she belonged. But he couldn't let her keep him from moving forward with his life.

Once he completed the bishop's addition, he would push all thoughts of Rainbow Girl from his mind. Her wild hair. Her odd clothes. Her sweet smile that made him happy.

He had to admit that he liked thinking about her.

But he shouldn't like it. Shouldn't think about her. He needed to stop. Right now.

Chapter Six

Eli arrived early the next morning alone. He'd told Daniel and Benjamin that he'd lay the concrete foundation blocks by himself since this part could be done in a day. Then the work would have to stop until an inspector came to sign off on the foundation. No sense taking up their time needlessly. He didn't mind spending most of the day here.

He glanced at the rear of the *dawdy haus*. Was Rainbow Girl up? Did she sleep late like a lot of *Englishers*? He hoped he'd get to see her today.

If he didn't have to wait for the inspector at various stages, this project could take a third of the time. After the foundation was inspected, the framing could go up and the electrical wired in. Once those were inspected, the rest of the job would progress without delay.

He combined the mortar and water in a wheelbarrow and set to work on the corners. He hoped to finish this addition by the middle of next week. Not only did he look forward to getting back to his regular routine at his forge, but he also figured that Rainbow Girl couldn't be all that comfortable sleeping on a couch. If she was going to stay, she needed her own space, and the sooner he finished, the sooner she would decide to stay. True, he wouldn't get to see her every day, but she would be in the community, and he could come up with excuses.

Ja. She needed to stay.

When the door opened, he looked up, and his breath caught in his throat.

Rainbow Girl stood in the doorway in the same bright green trousers and orange shirt as yesterday. She held a cup of something steamy. "Aren't the others helping you today?"

How pretty she would look in a cape dress and *kapp* again. He forced air into his lungs. "*Ne.* There's only enough work for one. They'll come to help put up the walls another day." If they were here, he wouldn't get to stay as long or see her as much.

"This is a lot for only one person."

"I can get it done by supper."

"I brought you a cup of coffee."

He set down his trowel and crossed to her. *"Danki."* He took the hot cup.

She smiled at him. "*Bitte.* The bishop and I are going into town."

"Why do you call him bishop instead of *grossvater*?"

She shrugged. "I guess since I was about ten or eleven, he always seemed more like the bishop than a *grossvater*."

He had a hard time imagining what it must be like to have the bishop as your *vater* or *grossvater*. "I need to pick up a few things for *meine mutter*. May I go with the two of you?"

She tilted her head in an adorable way and gave a winsome smile. "Then how will you finish here by supper?"

He glanced at the blocks all set out for the job to be done. "I'll manage."

"I'm sure the bish— *Meine grossvater* would be happy to have you along."

From somewhere behind her came "*Ja*. Come." The bishop appeared beside her. "We forgot to get the metal electric boxes for the outlets and switches."

"*Ja*, I was thinking about them last night. Would you like me to hitch up a buggy?"

"That would be *gut*. *Danki*. We'll take mine. It's the smaller enclosed one. Hitch Thunder to it."

"Very *gut*. I'll use up the rest of the mortar I have mixed and get to it." He downed the coffee that was still a bit too hot and handed the cup to Rainbow Girl. *"Danki."* He wouldn't be tasting any more food today.

On the bright side, he'd get to ride into town with Rainbow Girl seated next to him.

And that made him very happy.

Dori hadn't been able to squeeze into any of her regular pants, and she owned no skirts. She hadn't worn dresses or skirts since she'd left the Amish, so the options for her growing belly were limited. That meant settling for her teal yoga pants. They fitted snugly over her rounded stomach. She topped off the look with a coral-and-pink swirly patterned blouse that hung baggy over her hips, and her black knee boots. Not a great look for job hunting, but better than jeans or sweatpants for interviews. If she even managed to get any.

Sandwiched between the handsome young black-smith and her *grossvater*, a part of Dori delighted at sitting so close to Eli in the buggy. Another part of her harbored guilt for keeping her secret from him. But he really had no need to know about the baby. She would leave as soon as she could get a job and find a place to live.

About a mile into Goshen, Dori pointed. "Can you drop me off at the coffee shop on the corner?"

"Why?" The bishop gave her his squint-eyed expression when he looked into someone's soul.

What did he see in hers? "I don't think you want to know."

"I do."

She glanced at Eli, who seemed eager to know, as well. "I'm going to apply for a job there, and then use their Wi-Fi to look for other potential jobs."

Grossvater frowned. "You don't need a job."

She took a slow breath. It was a bit maddening. He refused to listen to anything she said. "I do if I'm going to rent a place in town."

"You don't need to do that. I'm building you two rooms."

She looked from the bishop to Eli. "See? He won't listen."

Eli scrunched his eyebrows together. "Two rooms?"

Her stomach flipped. How could she explain the extra space? "He's having you build two, and he wants me to live in one." She didn't need to explain to him who her *grossvater* hoped would occupy the other in a few months' time.

Eli pulled the buggy to a stop at a red light.

"I'll get out here." Dori stepped past her *grossvater*

and climbed down before either man could stop her. "*Danki.* I'll see you in an hour or so." She trotted up onto the sidewalk.

Once the buggy had pulled away, Dori glanced across the street to the sub shop, where Eli had bought her a sandwich. It seemed like so long ago, but it had been only three days. How bleak her life had seemed then. How different it was now. Her life had changed so quickly. From perfect with Craig, to dismal after he kicked her out, to...to nice? Comfortable? Secure? Right now, her life was all of the above, and she was glad of it.

Over an hour later, Dori arrived back at the coffee shop. Eli and the bishop were nowhere in sight, so she went inside. She'd talked to ten different businesses within walking distance, including the coffee shop, and ones she'd applied to online yesterday. She was given one of two answers. She either didn't have ample formal education—eighth grade wasn't enough—or they didn't want to hire someone in her condition. How could so many people tell she was pregnant? Had Eli figured it out as well and was he too polite to say anything?

Today's results had been proof enough that her chances of getting a job were very slim. Because of the numerous people looking for work, the job market was tough, and when the high school students got out for the summer, it would be even harder.

She should have tried harder to get her GED, but she hadn't seen a need while she was living with Craig. And in the Amish world, she never had to worry about that. She knew of a lot of people who'd been looking for work, long before she started. Long before Craig had kicked her out. Long before morning sickness had cost her the waitressing job. People with far more education than she had.

Should she give up on finding work altogether and wait until after the baby was born? If so, she either had to stay with the Amish or return to the homeless shelter. One option was slightly better than the other. But only slightly. How depressing.

This was not how she imagined her life when she left the Amish community. She imagined doing anything she wanted to do, but in reality, a person could do only what their education and resources allowed them. It seemed a lot like the limiting ways of the Amish. Not the total freedom she'd imagined.

She still had the ten dollars from Eli and ordered herself a berry smoothie. She missed having fancy coffees, mochas and lattes, but the caffeine wasn't *gut* for the baby. Sitting, she opened her laptop and quickly connected to the shop's Wi-Fi again. She would do as much as she could until the men showed up.

If she was going to get a job and an apartment, she needed to get her GED. That was how she'd spend her time until the baby arrived.

Before long, Eli strode in and headed her way. "Are you ready?"

Under the table, she slipped her hand to her belly. Had the baby moved in response to Eli's voice? Her heart had certainly reacted to his presence, and a feeling of *ja*-this-is-nice swept through her. "Let me check my email really fast." She clicked the keys.

The conversation from the next table was loud and Dori heard someone say, "There's something you don't see every day. An Amish man with a normal person."

Did they think they couldn't be heard? Dori laughed to herself. *She* was the normal one? Since when had her appearance been considered normal? She glanced up at Eli but couldn't tell if he'd heard them.

He spoke in a hushed voice loud enough for her ears only. "Ignore them."

That made her feel *gut*. He'd been trying to make her feel better. Protective, even. He had no way of knowing that the comment had made her laugh. Regardless, his gesture had been kind and touched her.

Craig would have turned on them and told them to mind their own business, after he'd scolded her for carrying her laptop in an unprotected bag rather than a specially designed padded one.

She closed her laptop and stowed it in her backpack. Before she could pick it up, Eli grabbed it and slung one strap over his shoulder. Sweet again. Was he doing it simply to be nice? Or had he been told she was pregnant?

She grabbed her smoothie, headed out to the buggy and sat between the men again. "Eli, did you get everything your *mutter* needed?"

He tipped his head back against the seat. "Oh, I forgot. It's only a few things. Do you mind if we stop again?"

"Of course not." *Grossvater* waved him on.

Eli parked the buggy at the big-box store. "I won't be long." He jumped down and ran in.

Though she might have liked to have gone in just to spend more time with him, she had the bishop alone. "Did you tell Eli about the baby?"

"*Ne.* That's for you to tell him. But you can't hide this much longer. Our people will want to help you."

"Like *Vater*?"

"Andrew is just hurt. He didn't forbid me to build the addition to the *dawdy haus* or really try to stop me. He told me I'm being a foolish old man, wasting *meine* time. When you get to *meine* age, the things that were once foolish aren't anymore. I think your *vater* truly hopes you'll stay."

Her *vater* hurt? He was too strong to let anything hurt him and certainly not her or her actions. How would Eli react when he found out about the baby? She wanted to keep it from him as long as possible, because when he did learn of it, he would likely react as her *vater* had.

Eli returned with a plastic shopping bag of items and a box of laundry soap. "*Danki* for waiting."

Once back at *Grossvater*'s *dawdy haus*, Eli went straight to work again after unhitching the horse. *Grossvater* worked alongside him.

On the kitchen table sat a plate of oatmeal cookies covered in plastic, and a note said that a large bowl of potato salad was in the refrigerator. With sandwiches, this would be a tasty lunch.

Dori made lunch-meat sandwiches with all the fixings and mixed up a pitcher of lemonade.

The June day had warmed up nicely but not too hot. Comfortable enough to work outdoors. She set the pitcher and glasses on the floor at the end of the hall, then added the bowl of potato salad with a serving spoon and forks, and returned for the three plates with sandwiches. She carried all of them with one hand and an arm, leaving her other hand free to open the door.

She froze and caught her breath. Eli carried a heavy bag of mortar mix on one shoulder. Had he always been that strong? Or had she simply never noticed? He was so brawny and manly. What would the *English* call him? A hunk. Amish never thought of the opposite sex in such a manner. Or at least, they never voiced it, but Eli Hochstetler was definitely a hunk. He probably had no idea how physically attractive he was, especially when he smiled. Add to that his kind heart and *gut* nature, and he was practically perfect. Except for the fact he was Amish, through and through.

He stopped next to the wheelbarrow where *Grossvater* stood. *Gut.* She was in time before they mixed more. If she could manage to cease her gawking. "Lunch."

After everyone had dished up their food and poured themselves a glass of lemonade, *Grossvater* said grace for their meal as well as the work ahead of them. Dori settled in the doorway, stealing glances at Eli. *Grossvater* sat on the bottom step, and Eli in the grass that would soon be under her floor.

The first to finish, Eli set his plate on one of the steps. *"Danki."*

Dori didn't want the time with him to be over. "I almost forgot." She sprang to her feet and dashed inside, then returned with the plate of cookies. *"Mutter* left these, as well as the potato salad." She held the plate out to Eli.

He took three and held them up. *"Danki."*

Grossvater took one. *"Ja, danki.* Your *mutter* makes the best cookies."

She liked thinking of him as *Grossvater.* It somehow made him seem kinder and more approachable.

After cleaning up lunch and washing the few dishes, Dori changed into gray sweatpants and a pink T-shirt, then headed outside to see if there was anything she could do. After all, she would be here until at least after the baby was born. She might as well make the best of it. She would start with lending assistance to build her rooms and pursuing her GED. The first allowed her to spend a bit more time with Eli.

Eli carried two concrete blocks over to the side wall of the foundation.

She looked around. "Where's *meine grossvater*?"

He set the blocks down. "He needed to visit a community member."

She strode over to him. "Then *gut* thing I'm here. What can I do?"

His eyebrows knit together. "Do with what?"

"Building the addition." *And spending time with you.*

His eyebrows inched up his forehead, and he laughed. "This is a man's work."

That's right. Amish men built things, and Amish women cooked and cleaned. If she'd stuck to that rule, half the light bulbs in her and Craig's apartment would be out, the bathroom cabinet door would still be leaning against the wall, and the garbage disposal broken and backed up with decaying food particles. It was amazing what she'd learned from online videos. "I'm capable of doing plenty. You lost all that time going into town, and now your one helper has abandoned you."

He shook his head and headed for the block pile again. "Go back inside."

"You think me incapable?" She hurried around in front of him, not wanting to be readily dismissed. "I'll have you know that I've wielded a screwdriver and wrench a time or two."

He laughed. "Neither of which are used in masonry."

"I know that. They were examples to show you I'm capable."

He folded his arms.

Stubborn man.

A manly man.

And handsome.

A hunk.

She folded her arms too. "I'm not leaving. This addition is for me, and I'm going to help. Wouldn't you rather put me to work? Or have me get in your way? The choice is yours."

He huffed out a breath. "Fine. You can mix the mortar." He hefted a bag of dry cement, cut it open across the middle with his trowel and dumped the contents into the wheelbarrow, sending up a cloud of powder.

She waved her hand in front of her face to clear the air.

He added water from the hose, handed her a hoe and walked away. Not one word of instruction.

But what instruction did she really need? *Mix*. She pulled the hoe back and forth to blend the wet and dry ingredients. Not much different than combining the makings for a cake. "How will I know when it's ready?"

"I'll tell you." He grabbed more blocks. With each pair he transferred, he glanced into the wheelbarrow. A couple of times, he added more water.

The mixing turned out to be a lot harder than she'd anticipated. Mortar was heavy, and the process caused her muscles to cry out, but she didn't dare complain. Soon she would have a nice place to live—her own space. And it was a bonus that she got to spend time with Eli. Just the two of them.

A little bit later, after she'd watched his methodology, she knew how to be of further assistance. She could cut his per-block time in half by handing them to him. While he slapped the mortar in place, she gripped one and heaved. It was all she could do to raise it an inch off the ground. These were heavier than she thought. She didn't want to hurt her back, so she crouched. She still couldn't lift it.

"What are you doing?"

She tilted her head and squinted up at him. "Helping. How much do each of these weigh?"

He shook his head. "Not much. Thirty-five or forty pounds." He grabbed the block she'd been trying to lift and hoisted it with one hand as though it was nothing more than his dinner plate. "Don't try to lift another one of these."

She wanted to protest, but what was the point? They both knew she couldn't, even if she wanted to, so she studied him instead.

The way he applied the mortar in swift motions, never hesitating, mesmerized her. Scoop, splat mortar into place on an already set block, scoop-splat, scoop-swish-swish mortar on the end of the next block and set it in place.

By suppertime, the foundation walls were completed. The room that would be built on top was already welcoming her.

Eli wiped his hands on a rag. "*Danki*. It went much faster with your help."

"And what help would that be? Watching?"

"Mixing the mortar."

"That didn't take much time."

"But it allowed me do other things, so the work went faster."

Her insides danced at his praise. "It did?"

"Ja."

She wasn't sure if that was the truth or if he was merely being nice. Then a smile pulled at her mouth. Of course it was true. She'd never known Eli to lie. But that he admitted it to her was amazing. He could have easily said nothing, leaving her to believe she hadn't made a difference at all.

Dori wasn't the only one who had changed from her Amish roots. Perhaps her influence had set Eli on his own path, cracking the traditions and helping him to soften the rigid ways.

Working beside him had been rewarding. She'd enjoyed the time, and she decided that she would help with the whole addition, whether he approved or not. She could be just as stubborn as any of the men.

What was it about Eli that made her feel happier than she'd been in a long time? And there was something safe in being near him. Both things she definitely wanted to hold on to.

Chapter Seven

The next morning, Dori sat at the table eating a bowl of Oaty-Ohs mixed with Cinna-Apple Rings. She had enjoyed working with Eli yesterday, though her muscles were telling a different story today. She wouldn't see him for a few days, maybe not until next week. It all depended on when the inspector came to look over what had been done on the addition so far.

Grossvater entered through the front door from wherever he'd been. "I have a favor to ask of you."

"What is it, *Grossvater*?"

"Eli's not coming today because the construction has to wait until the foundation is inspected. I had planned to take Nelly to his forge—she's thrown a shoe—but I'm needed on the far side of the district. Are you up to walking Nelly over to Eli's for me?"

"The exercise will do me—us—*gut*." She caressed her stomach. "We'd love to." She would enjoy seeing Eli at his forge, sending a little thrill through her at the prospect. In truth, the prospect of not seeing Eli had saddened her. "Shouldn't I wait for the inspector?" Now that she'd realized that she had to stay, at least until the baby was born, she was anxious for the extra rooms to be finished.

"*Ne*, the inspection card is attached to the back door. Are you sure the walk won't be too much for you?"

"We'll be fine."

"*Danki*. I need to leave. Can you get Nelly all right?"

"*Ja, Grossvater*. I haven't forgotten everything about being Amish." Not that she *was* Amish or ever would be. Despite the fact that she had fully assimilated into the *Englisher* world, that hadn't erased her past. Everything came back to her like an old friend.

His wide grin and the mischievous twinkle in his eyes suggested *Grossvater* might be up to something. He slipped out before she could question him.

Was he trying to get her to interact with the community? Maybe he thought if he got her more involved with the Amish people in the community she would stay, but he was wrong. However, she did like the chance to get out of the *haus*.

Dori had chosen to wear yoga pants that morning. Not only were they comfortable on her growing waistline, but they had a back pocket, which was convenient for carrying her cell phone. She slipped it in there and then headed for the barn. On her way, she glanced toward the big *haus*. *Mutter* was likely in there alone, cleaning up the kitchen.

In the barn, Dori bridled Nelly and walked her outside. How long would it take to get to Eli's?

Mutter met her outside the barn and held up a canvas shopping bag. "Cookies for you and Eli."

"How did you know where I was headed?"

"Your *grossvater* told me. I also packed sandwiches—egg salad. You always liked egg salad. And some cheese, in case you get hungry on your way there or back. I know I had to eat often when I was pregnant with all you children."

Hunger had become Dori's constant companion, but at least now she knew she would have food to eat. The bowl of cold cereal wouldn't last her long. She took the bag from her *mutter*. "*Danki*. But you aren't supposed to be talking to me."

"You aren't shunned, so it's all right."

A technicality. "What about *Vater*?"

"He won't mind."

"Meaning you're not going to tell him." For all the Amish rules, people bent them often enough to suit their needs or wants.

"He saw you working alongside Eli yesterday. He's glad you're home."

Mutter probably just hoped he was glad. "Could have fooled me."

"*Ja*, well, it was a shock—" *Mutter* dipped her head "—seeing you."

Dori *was* quite an odd sight in an Amish community with her colorful hair and *Englisher* clothes.

"I left your Amish clothes on the porch the first morning."

As Dori had suspected, her own clothes had come back to haunt her. "I found them." The ones she'd stuffed safely away in the corner of the living room, where *Grossvater* wouldn't know to ask her about them.

"If you wore them, your *vater* would yield more quickly."

Her *mutter* wanted—*ne*, needed—everyone to be at peace with each other.

"I'll think about it, but I won't make any promises." A shiver tingled her skin in agitation merely thinking about putting on a cape dress again.

"*Danki.* I can't ask for anything more. You best be on your way, before the *morgen* gets away from you."

Poor *Mutter.* She wanted what she couldn't have. Her family to be whole again and everyone happy. To have one, excluded the other.

Dori headed off down the road toward the Hochstetler farm. An hour later, after she'd eaten half the cheese, she entered the yard.

The clang of Eli's hammer rang through the air.

She walked the horse around to the back of the barn where Eli's forge stood, open like a two-car garage. She stopped a few yards from the large threshold.

He swung his hammer onto red-hot metal. Sparks sprayed up in all directions from the contact point. His actions were smooth and practiced, no wasted motions. Almost as though he worked to some internal rhythm. He looked as though he'd stepped out of a blacksmith calendar. She'd buy that calendar. Especially if all the pictures featured the handsome Eli.

The piece took shape as he worked and worked. An herb chopper. So that was how he fashioned one of those. A table along the rear wall behind the forge fire held many pieces of ironwork. Kitchen knives, cooking utensils, fireplace tools, ax heads, weather vanes and various other items she couldn't identify from this distance.

Nelly whinnied and pawed the ground, evidently not enjoying the view as much as Dori.

Eli looked up, and a smile lit up his face. "Rain—

Dor— *Hallo.*" He shoved the iron piece he'd been working into the hot coals. "Does Nelly need a shoe?"

Again, her baby responded to Eli's voice, moving around inside her. "How did you know?"

"Usual reason people come unannounced, walking a horse." He ambled over and stroked the draft horse's neck. "How are you doing, Nelly?"

The horse lipped his shoulder.

"Do you know all the horses in the community by name?"

He shrugged. "There are a few new ones I don't. Yet."

"You called me Rain a moment ago. Why?"

His face turned red and not from the hot fire. "Which hoof?" Without waiting for an answer, he went straight to the hind leg and lifted it.

He had to have heard her question, but she would play his game. She pointed at Nelly's leg. "How did you know which one?"

"She had her hind hoof cocked up."

"You certainly know horses."

"Horses are part of *meine* job. They're easy to figure out."

"Easier than people?"

He nodded. "Everything about them conveys something. The different sounds they make. The way they stand, the tilt of their ears, the swish of their tail. Horses have much to communicate."

She'd never thought that much about horses. In her youth, she viewed them as a means to pull buggies and plows. In the *Englisher* world, they were a source of irritation by impeding traffic and leaving smelly things on the road to avoid.

He took the lead rope and walked Nelly over to a post and secured her there. With his tools, he cleaned out the hoof, then set it on a hoof rest and filed it. With various shoe sizes, he measured until he found one that was close and shoved it into his coals with a pair of long tongs. "This will take a few minutes. Do you want a chair?"

She was a bit worn-out from the walk. *"Ja, danki."*

He grabbed a three-legged stool and plopped it down in front of her, well outside the danger zone of getting hit by flying sparks. "You'll be safe here." With the extra long tongs, he moved the metal shoe around in the coals, digging it deeper in the heat.

She instinctively put a hand on her stomach as she sat, then quickly removed it. "So tell me, why did you call me Rain?"

He shook his head. "It was nothing."

"I want to know."

He pulled the shoe out, studied it and shoved it back in. "I used to see you in town every time I went. I didn't know who you were, so I called you…"

"Rain?"

"Rainbow Girl." He pointed toward her head with the long tongs. "On account of your colorful mane."

She ran a hand through her cropped hair. "I kind of like that. You can call me Rainbow Girl. It's a lot better than *Dorcas*."

"Dorcas is a nice name."

"I don't really like it. It doesn't suit me. So either call me Dori or Rainbow Girl. Or just plain Rainbow."

Rather than agreeing, he pulled the shoe from the fire and beat on it, sending sparks into the air again.

She stood and scooted around him to the table with his wares.

He stopped his work. "What are you doing?"

"I want to look at all the pieces you've made."

He put the shoe back into the coals and stood next to her. "Just things I make when I'm caught up on *meine* other work."

She jerked her hand from her stomach again. She needed to stop doing that. Soon enough she would show too much to hide her growing belly with a baggy shirt. She should probably tell him soon.

Besides the pieces she could see from a distance, a six-inch-tall deer sat among various other animals. She picked up an iron frog not much bigger than a real frog. "These are really nice."

"*Danki.* You can have it." He returned to the horseshoe.

"Really?"

"*Ja.* As you can see, I have plenty."

She peered over her shoulder at him and slipped her cell phone out of her back pocket. She took pictures of everything, trying to get as close to each object as she could and still keep it in focus with the limited light. When she finished, she sat down again and inconspicuously snapped a few pictures of Eli. These would look great on his website, him wielding a hammer with sparks flying. Nothing that gave the appearance of him posing, because that would not be fitting.

She smiled. The website he didn't have—her smile widened—but soon would.

Eli struck the iron in an unusual cadence, his normal rhythm off. He couldn't believe Rainbow Girl was here, and he'd been taken aback to have her suddenly standing there. His focus returned to the horseshoe.

Completely misshapen. Ruined.

He tossed it into the water barrel and took another mostly formed shoe from the wall. He wedged it into the fire with the long tongs and worked the bellows. He made shoes ahead of time in various sizes so horses and their owners didn't have to wait so long.

What was Rainbow Girl doing with her phone? Still too much *English*. Would she ever settle back into the Amish way of life? Doubtful. She had said herself that she didn't know if she would stay. But she'd helped him finish the foundation of the addition rather than trying to talk him out of it like before. She almost seemed eager to have the project completed. Was that because she wanted to be rid of him? He hoped not, but when he finished, even if she stayed in their community, he wouldn't see her as often. Only on Church Sundays. If she went at all.

He took his time sizing the shoe and filing Nelly's hoof. He didn't want Rainbow Girl to leave. He cleaned out each hoof.

"Are you almost done?"

Was she so anxious to be away from him? "I want to make sure she has a *gut* fit."

Rainbow Girl held up the cloth bag she'd brought. "Well, when you're done, I have lunch for us."

He nailed the shoe into place, turned Nelly out into the corral, then grabbed a blanket, his tin drinking cup and a jug of water. "The shade on the side of the barn will be more comfortable." He let her walk ahead of him.

He set the jug and cup down, and she did the same with her bag. She took two corners of the blanket and helped him spread it out. They worked well together as they had yesterday, when she'd helped with the foundation, as though they knew what the other was going to do. It made the day's work go faster. With the delay of going into town, he'd accepted he would have to work through supper until dark, or return the next day to finish, therefore holding up the inspection.

He gave her a hand to sit on the blanket, then he sat, as well. The egg salad sandwiches were loaded with lettuce, tomatoes and onions. Just the way he liked them. "Did you make these?"

"*Ne, meine mutter* did."

He'd hoped Rainbow Girl had prepared lunch, then he could compliment her. "Tell her everything was delicious and *danki*."

"I will."

After eating, Eli led Dutch, harnessed to the two-wheeled trap, out of the barn. Rainbow Girl stood some distance away. Eyes closed, face tilted toward the blue sky, one hand on her lower back and the other on her round stomach. She wasn't a horse, so what did *her* stance communicate?

Then his breath got knocked out of him as though a mule had kicked him.

Rainbow Girl couldn't be pregnant!

But it all made sense, her return to the community, and her *vater* being so upset with her instead of welcoming his prodigal daughter home. How could Eli have allowed her to help him with construction? *Gut* thing he'd stopped her from lifting those heavy concrete blocks.

Where was the baby's *vater*? Was he coming for them? He was probably the reason she insisted she wasn't staying. She was using her Amish family. Her *vater* knew, but did the rest of them? Did the bishop? Would he be so welcoming if he did?

Rainbow Girl straightened and turned toward him. She adjusted her shirt, apparently to hide her condition, and walked toward him. "Is everything all right, Eli? You look upset."

"I'm fine." He released the harness and set the brake on the rig. "I'll get Nelly." After striding to the corral, he gripped the top rail and squeezed it as hard as he could, making the rough wood bite into his palms.

He'd thought she might have actually wanted to change her ways, to return to the Amish life, to be the woman *Gott* intended her to be. How could he have let her get under his skin?

Nelly stuck her muzzle over the railing and into his face.

"Did you know?" he asked the sweet mare.

The draft horse stared at him with soulful brown eyes.

"Come on, girl. Time to go home." He walked into the corral and bridled the gentle giant. He no longer wanted to drive Rainbow Girl home or spend time with her, but he couldn't allow her to walk all that way back home. Having lived with the *Englishers* so long and driven everywhere in cars, she'd likely grown soft. He led Nelly out of the corral and toward the buggy. Maybe he'd seen wrong. Maybe the light had played tricks on him. Maybe...

He tied the horse to the rear of the trap.

Rainbow Girl had already climbed in. She should not have done that on her own. What if she slipped and hurt herself or the baby?

He hoisted himself up, took hold of the reins and put the buggy into motion.

"*Danki* for taking *gut* care of Nelly."

"*Ja.*" He glanced repeatedly out of the corner of his eye, trying to confirm if she was pregnant.

After a mile, she said, "Is everything all right?"

Ne, not at all. "Why wouldn't it be?"

"You're really quiet."

His mind wasn't. It was racing with chaotic thoughts and emotions. The drive couldn't end quickly enough for him.

He dropped her off in front of the *dawdy haus.*

"I'll get Nelly so you can be on your way."

"*Ne.* I'll do it." He drove toward the barn before she could untie the horse.

"*Danki* for the ride," she called after him.

He waved his hand over his head to let her know he'd heard her. In the barn, he secured Nelly in her stall and hurried back outside.

Bishop Bontrager met up with him at the trap. "*Danki* for taking care of Nelly."

"I'm glad to help."

"The inspector came and signed the card."

"I'll return in the *morgen. Guten tag.*" Eli snapped the reins before he could be delayed again.

Rainbow Girl was pregnant. Would she stay until the baby was born? No wonder her *vater* would have nothing to do with her. Eli wanted nothing to do with her either, but it was too late.

He had time to build. He'd given his word freely to the bishop that he'd build the addition. He had a strong back and skilled hands. He gave that too to the bishop, with no resentment.

But Rainbow Girl had wiggled her way into his heart. Without permission. With no recourse on his part. That he did resent, and he would need to excise her from his heart as well as his thoughts.

Strangely, he blamed his own foolishness. Little blame fell on the one who had wronged her family, her community, her *Gott*. He thought of Rainbow Girl and felt a protective need to shield her. Was she shaking his faith? Was she going to be an obstruction between *Gott* and himself? This could not be. He had no intention of following Rainbow Girl into the *Englisher* world. But Rainbow Girl had brought the *Englisher* world to their community in a way that could not be ignored.

But just because *she* returned didn't mean anything for him had changed. He was still in need of a wife. On his way home, he pulled into the Miller farm and asked to speak to Miriam. Her smile made her subsequent refusal seem like a sweet gift.

Her rejection stung, but not like it should. More because of the blow to his ego and less because he cared so much for her that he felt an actual loss. He was more upset he couldn't show Rainbow Girl his life was fulfilling and on track without her.

But it wasn't. It never had been.

And that stung even more.

Chapter Eight

The next day, Dori woke to the sounds of hammers and men's voices outside. She dressed and ate quickly. Since it seemed as though she was going to stay with her *grossvater* for the time being, she exited through the back door, determined to do what she could to make this project go as fast as possible.

Eli, Daniel and Benjamin bustled around the interior of the foundation. They had started early and wasted no time on capping the top of the concrete blocks with wood, and had three floor joists in place already. She'd forgotten how fast Amish men could build things.

She stepped down onto the grass. *"Guten morgen."*

Eli looked up from hoisting a two-by-twelve. He narrowed his eyes at her and dropped the board. "Take a break." He strode to her like a ram toward an intruder.

Dori held her ground and smiled. "How can I help today?"

He gritted his teeth. "Go back inside."

"Ne. I want to do something."

"Ne. Go. Inside."

She planted her hands on her hips. "I'm going to help, whether you approve or not."

He stood in her path. "I won't allow you out here."

Why was he acting like this? He'd let her help him the other day. Was it because there were other men around? Would his manly pride get bruised? "You can't stop me, Eli Hochstetler."

He lowered his voice. "It's not *gut* for the baby."

The blood drained from her face. "How long have you known?"

"Since yesterday. Does the bishop know?"

"Of course. How did you...?"

"Just go inside and don't come out again." He walked away.

She stumbled back into the house and closed the door. Tears spilled down her cheeks. The hurt in his expression wrenched her heart. She should have told him herself, but she'd wanted to revel in the nice friendship they were rekindling. Letting him figure it out on his own had been a grave error in judgment. It had happened right before he'd brought her home. She realized that now. How could she have been so careless? How could she ever make amends?

She slumped into a chair at the table and opened her laptop. Last night, she'd gotten Eli a buddy page connected to another Amish website. Which meant that he wouldn't have to pay for a domain until he was ready. She would show him what his website could be. She would make it up to him for not telling him about the baby. Just because he wouldn't let her do anything further to help build the addition didn't mean she couldn't help him in some other way.

She connected her cell phone to the laptop and

downloaded the pictures she'd taken yesterday. Within an hour, she had a basic site ready for content. She did her best to write about each item. Eli could help her fine-tune the descriptions later. All of Craig's instructions about graphics and web design had paid off. She hadn't realized how much she'd learned.

At the end of the day, she had the bare bones of a website built. And the three-man construction team had the skeletal walls of the *dawdy haus* addition up, with the electrical wired in and the floor joists in place. They also had managed to finish the roof, complete with shingles and gutters. Everything ready for the next inspection. Eli wouldn't return for a day or two, and she wanted to show him what she'd accomplished. She stepped out the back door onto the small stoop. Her sister stood talking to Daniel Burkholder. "Eli, may I speak with you a moment?"

He didn't turn to her right away as the other two young men and her sister did, but when he did, the scowl on his face spoke loudly of his irritation.

Well, let him be irritated. He would change his mood when he saw his website. Now he wouldn't have to hire a *Englisher* to build it for him. That would save him money, and Amish were all about frugality.

He huffed out a breath. "What? It's been a long day, and I want to get home."

What he meant was he wanted to get away from her. He probably regretted ever agreeing to help the bishop.

"Would you come here, please? Unless you'd like me to go over there."

He crawled over the foundation and walked between the floor joists to her. "What?"

"Come inside."

"I don't want to. Just tell me what it is."

"I can't. I have to show you." She walked down the hall, hoping he would follow her. And he did. When he caught up to her, she pointed toward her computer. "Look. I made you a website."

He sat and stared at the screen.

"Click around." When he didn't move, she reached in front of him and changed the screen to one of his pieces, a weather vane. She drew in a deep breath. He smelled of wood and smoke. She wanted to lean into the aromas but resisted. If he was angry now, that would upset him even more. "I didn't know quite how to describe the items you make—the correct terminology and all—but you can help me with that. This is merely a temporary site until you can buy a domain name."

He stood. "I told you I didn't want you to do this. Undo it."

His rejection stung. Why wasn't he pleased?

"But this is the best way for you to get orders from *English* customers and make more money. You don't want an *Englisher* in charge of your website. You need to learn this yourself."

He walked back down the hall. "Undo it, I said."

Dori put her hands on her hips. Stubborn man. He could protest all he wanted, but in the end, who wouldn't want a website created for free? Did he realize how much an outsider would charge? A lot. When he cooled down, he'd see that this was a *gut* thing. He would see that she was right. If he still hated what she'd done in a day or two, she would take it down.

Maybe.

She could be stubborn too.

* * *

On Saturday night, Dori sat at her *grossvater*'s table and bowed her head as he said a blessing over the meal she'd cooked. Dried-out chicken with half-raw and half-burnt fried potatoes. It wasn't that she couldn't cook, but her mind kept wandering back to Eli's words when he'd acknowledged that he knew about her baby and his vehement refusal of the website she'd created for him. Something inside her needed him to approve of her work. Approve of her. But he likely never would.

The bishop said, "Amen." He raised his head and picked up his fork.

Dori grabbed hers as well and stabbed a blackened potato chunk. "Sorry about the potatoes."

"They're fine."

They weren't. With the raw and burnt bits aside, the rest of the flavor wasn't bad.

He swallowed a bite of chicken and chased it with a swig of milk. "I have a favor to ask of you."

Dori had a bad feeling about this. "What is it?"

"I want you to come to the big *haus* with me tomorrow morning for family church."

Had she already been here for a week? "I don't think that's a *gut* idea. *Vater* wouldn't like that."

"It will show him you are trying."

But she wasn't. Not really. But she also wasn't actively trying to leave. If she hadn't lost her job, she wouldn't be here. If Craig hadn't kicked her out, she wouldn't be here. If she had been able to find new work, she wouldn't be here. But none of those were likely to change, and life here wasn't as bad as she'd imagined. "I'll think about it." It might actually be pleasant, and she couldn't afford to have *Grossvater* kick her out too.

"And services the other Sundays, as well." He rolled his eyes toward the ceiling.

A reminder that he was providing the roof over her head?

She nodded.

"And would you mind removing the jewelry from your face and ears? It would be distracting for the younger ones."

There it was. Get her to agree to one seemingly benign thing and then ask for more. "Next, you'll want me to wear a cape dress."

"That wouldn't hurt."

She folded her arms on the table. "I'll go tomorrow, and I'll even take out the piercings in *meine* face, but not *meine* ears. And I'm *not* wearing a cape dress."

"What about your hair?"

He was going to push this to see how much she would give.

"It stays the way it is." Brown roots and all. It actually looked pretty awful with it half her natural color and half-multicolored. A few inches longer and someone could mistake it for being intentionally colored on the ends. If she had the money, she would recolor the roots.

Grossvater pressed his lips together.

After a couple of dry, hard-to-swallow bites, Dori had an idea. He wasn't the only one with a wish list. "*Grossvater*, I think you should get internet service and a computer. Before you object, let me explain."

He narrowed his eyes. "I have a feeling I won't like this, but continue."

"So many Amish have websites as a necessity for their businesses to survive. I think it would be a *gut* idea if you had internet and a computer so you could check up on them and monitor their sites." While giving her more reliable service to earn her GED and update Eli's site.

"I don't know how to work a computer."

"I will teach you."

He shook his head. "I don't wish to learn."

Just like Eli.

"One more thing, Dorcas. I want you to take the membership classes."

Changing the subject on her? "I'm not joining church, *Grossvater*."

"I won't make you. That decision is between you and *Gott*." He shrugged. "But what would it hurt to sit through the classes? The teacher is quite *gut*." He gave an impish grin.

The teacher being the bishop sitting across from her.

Two could play at this game. Dori leaned forward. "Here's the deal. I remove the piercings from *meine* face, but not the ones in *meine* ears. No cape dress, but I'll wear less...colorful clothes, black sweatpants and a plain top in a prescribed Amish color. I'll wear a black beanie hat to disguise *meine* hair. I'll attend church on Sundays." She swallowed hard. "And I'll attend the membership classes, *but* I'm not joining."

"Wunderbar." He thought he'd won.

She held up her hand. "I'm not done. I'll do these things in exchange for you getting internet service, a computer and approving a website for Eli." She could be just as stubborn as the men.

He frowned at her.

She held out her hand across the table. "Deal?" As much as she wanted these things for herself, in truth they would help him keep track of what his flock did with technology and make sure people used it as it had been approved for each individual. She knew the secrets of the Amish better than the bishop, and, like *Englishers*, they tried to get away with things, like hiding forbidden technology in their barns or cupboards. Being the bishop, he wasn't privy to his flock's secret actions. Most infractions weren't bad or serious, but the internet had the potential for real wickedness. If he knew all that cyberspace contained, no one would ever gain approval for a computer again.

He folded his arms. "You have learned some bad habits living with the *English*."

He hadn't even begun to see all of her "bad habits."

Her hand still hovered in the air between them.

He nodded and, surprisingly, shook her hand. "You are a tough haggler."

"Danki, Grossvater." Now, if she could just convince Eli. The following morning, Dori regretted agreeing to attend the family service. Her *vater*'s disapproving looks were offset by her *mutter*'s compassionate ones. Strained silence and awkward glances dominated the gathering. It was grueling. Worse than Dori had imagined. Worse yet was when the bishop forced her to tell her brothers that she was pregnant.

Matthew glared at her, while her three youngest brothers stared wide-eyed.

She wanted to flee. Instead, she distracted herself by pressing the tip of her tongue against the hole in her lip. It felt odd to not have the stud there, scraping on her tooth. She would replace it as soon as she returned to the *dawdy haus*. She'd promised to remove them for services but not permanently. She didn't want the holes to close up.

But maybe Eli wouldn't look so disapprovingly on her if she left them out.

Chapter Nine

The inspector arrived late on Tuesday afternoon, so Eli and the others wouldn't resume building until Wednesday. Eli had hoped to complete the room this week. Though he loved working in his forge, he strangely looked forward to this project, which surprised him. He also didn't want to see Rainbow Girl but at the same time did. He'd contemplated several girls he might ask to court, but in the end, he gave up the idea because his heart wasn't in it.

He drove the wagon up next to the corral. "You two get started. I'll take care of the horse and wagon."

Daniel and Benjamin jumped down and headed across the grass.

It would do Eli *gut* to put off seeing her for a few more minutes. Give him a chance to collect his thoughts and prepare himself for her ostentatious appearance. He unhitched the horse. Even mentally preparing himself, Rainbow Girl's appearance startled him every time.

With the horse taken care of, he headed for the construction site.

Rainbow Girl stood in the grass between the floor joists, talking with Daniel and Benjamin.

How had Eli missed her being pregnant? It seemed so obvious now.

Daniel had his arms folded. "I don't think you belong here."

"You're right, but I'm here, for better or for worse."

Where was the bishop? He needed to keep Rainbow Girl out of sight.

Eli marched toward them, climbed over the foundation wall and narrowed his eyes at her. "May I speak with you a moment?"

"Don't worry, I'm not going to do anything dangerous."

He spoke through gritted teeth. "Now." He motioned toward the back door.

She took a slow, deep breath, held it a moment and released it just as slowly. "Okay." She swiveled toward the *haus* and trudged up the steps and inside. Once in the kitchen area, she whirled around. "What? I don't appreciate you ordering me about."

"Too bad. You can't be outside. What if one of them realizes you're expecting?"

"I'm not going to be able to hide it much longer, and it's not going to matter in a few days anyway. *Meine grossvater* has decided to tell the whole church on Sunday." She waved her arm through the air. "He thinks it's best if everyone knows, so they can *help* me."

He didn't want the bishop to do that. Rainbow Girl would be singled out. If the bishop announced this, it would make it real. He wanted to protect her from the ridicule. "If the bishop has decided, then I guess it's done." He turned to head outside again, then swung back. "Please stay in the *haus*."

She tilted her head and pressed her lips together.

A sinking feeling in his gut told him she wasn't likely to obey. "You're a distraction." Mostly to him. "Just stay out of sight of the construction, then."

"I can't make any promises. *Grossvater* told me to see to it that you boys are fed. Can't very well bring you food if I'm not allowed to be seen."

He pressed his lips together. "I'm not a *boy*." Was that how she thought of him? Still the boy from school days?

"Whatever."

In spite of being mildly irritated, he enjoyed this banter, but the sound of plywood sheets being moved on top of the floor joists reminded him that he had a job to do, so he moved to leave again.

"Oh, wait, Eli."

He glanced over his shoulder. "I have a room to finish for you. *Ne*, two rooms."

"*Ja*. But that's not what I wanted to say. It's about that website I made you."

"I told you to undo it."

She paused a moment, biting her bottom lip. "I didn't quite get to that."

He should be irked at her but found he wasn't, which irritated him even more. "Well, do it now."

"Here's the problem." She held up a hand with her fingers splayed. "You already have five orders."

He stared hard at her, trying to process what she'd said. "I what?"

"Five customers have asked to purchase some of your items."

"They have?" He couldn't believe it. "That fast?"

"Ja." She sat at the table and tapped on her computer, then she swiveled it to face him. "An herb chopper—I think that's going to be a *gut* seller for you—an ax head, a weather vane and two animals."

He leaned in toward the screen. "That's too much money. I sell them for less."

"Not anymore. I checked competitors' prices, and these are right in the middle. The *English* will pay these prices and more for Amish-made items. I need to create your online payment account, so you can receive their payments and ship them their orders."

"I don't know how to do that." One of the many things he needed to learn how to do this summer.

"That's what you have me for. I've already told each of them that we are currently having a little problem with our payment system and will notify them as soon as we have the issue resolved."

"We?"

"Unless you'll be doing it, I'll be fixing the issue, so it's kind of a we thing at this point."

Incredible. She'd been home for only a week and a half and already she had orders for him. It had taken him all spring to sell that many pieces by consigning them to various shops around the community and in town. She'd gotten his business going quickly. Gratitude edged out his ire.

"You'll need a checking account to get an online payment system set up. You also need to name your business and purchase the domain name."

This was too much. He didn't understand this computer and website stuff. He didn't want to. He just wanted to make things in his forge. He'd dreaded spending the summer learning how to do all this, but now, he thought, maybe he wouldn't have to. "Would you help me with everything?"

"Of course."

"I'll pay you."

"Let's call it a fair trade for building me half of a *haus*."

He straightened. "Speaking of building a *haus*, I need to get to work."

"We should get all this sorted out soon. You don't want to lose these customers and get any negative feedback."

"I could return after supper."

"You don't need to leave and return. You can eat with us. It'll save a lot of time."

"Ja." He hurried outside, thinking about working alongside Rainbow Girl later. He'd like that. He'd like that a lot.

During the remainder of the afternoon, his mind spent more time on Rainbow Girl and his website than construction.

"Eli, lift your end," Daniel called out.

Eli refocused on the job at hand, but she was never far from his thoughts.

Since no progress could be made on construction earlier that week until after the inspector had come a second time, Dori had taken *Grossvater* into town on Monday to purchase a laptop and get internet service installed. So by Wednesday evening, she had everything in place to help Eli get his payment system set up. This new computer was so much faster than Craig's old castoff.

Grossvater sat in his brown recliner, napping, while Eli sat in a chair nestled close to hers at the table so he could watch the computer screen while she worked. So close his arm touched hers, sending jolts through her every now and then. She'd imagined what this would be like, but reality turned out to be so much better. She should adjust her position to create a couple of inches between them but enjoyed the innocent contact too much.

Eli fingered the side of the screen. "I can't believe you talked the bishop into purchasing a computer."

"It's so he can keep watch over his flock."

He furrowed his eyebrows at her. "And he believed that?"

"Fine. I wanted better internet, but it's still a *gut* idea for him to keep tabs on what his people are up to."

"Sort of like teaching a cat to swim?"

She shrugged. "Now, watch what I'm doing." Struggling to concentrate on the task at hand and not on the handsome man next to her, she explained her way through the process. "Does all that make sense?"

"Not a word."

"Aren't you learning anything?"

He shrugged this time.

"Then why are you sitting with me?"

"A pretty girl told me I had to. Told me I should learn about computers, but I have no interest when she'll do it for me."

Pretty? He thought she was pretty? "You would rather be in your forge, wouldn't you?"

"Not necessarily."

That answer surprised her. So he sat here because he wanted to be near her and not because he had to. He had a strong enough stubborn streak to have refused her request if he had a mind to. She liked working beside him. "Let's set up your payment system now. Do you have your checking account information?"

Like most Amish, he had a bank account. It was hard to do business with *Englishers* without one. Unless Amish wanted to walk around with bags of cash, they needed safe ways to transfer money to pay for the items they needed—and wanted.

He pulled his checkbook from his back pocket. He'd ended the construction day a little early so he could run home to retrieve it after dropping off Daniel and Benjamin at their homes.

She swiveled the laptop to face him. "Now, do as I tell you."

"I don't think I want to." He pushed the laptop toward her. "Why don't you just do it? It'll be faster. I don't want to click on the wrong thing."

"Because, as a businessman, you need to learn." And she wasn't going to be here forever. He needed to be self-sufficient.

"I never wanted to be a businessman, only a blacksmith."

"If you want to make a living smithing, you need to have some business skills, then you can continue to be a blacksmith."

He gave a playful groan. "Fine. What do I do?"

She moved the laptop in front of him and walked him through, step-by-step, setting up the online system. "You did great. Now, let's get it connected to your temporary site, inform your customers you're ready to receive payments, get you a domain name, transfer your website content to it and market your work on social media."

He stood abruptly and stepped away. "I have to do *all* that? I thought I only had to set up the payment thing. I've had enough for one day. I'll do it tomorrow or the next day."

"You could lose these sales and get negative feedback, which could damage your chances for future sales." She held her hand out to him. "Sit down. I'll do it for you, and you can watch." The poor man had to be overwhelmed with all there was to take in. She understood. She'd felt the same way when Craig had first tried to teach her about computers. With her new-found knowledge over the past four years, she didn't know how the Amish managed without computers in the modern age.

"I don't care about feedback and all that other stuff."

He did, but he didn't know it yet. All that stuff would allow him to do what he loved. "Sit. I'll talk through it as I do all the *stuff*. You watch."

He took a deep breath and sat. "I thought the computer stuff would be..."

"Simpler?"

He nodded. "And less of it. How does anyone know how to do it all?"

"They learn a little at a time, and you can learn it too. I'm sorry for overwhelming you with so much at once."

"I feel as though I'll never have time to work with the iron."

"I'll get you started, then it won't take as much time to keep it up. While I set things up, you be thinking of a name for your business. I chose *Eli's Amish Ironworks*,

but you need to choose something you like, and we'll
see if we can get you that domain name."

"What about just *Ironworks*? Simple. No extrane-
ous words."

Plain and simple, the Amish way. "It's a little *too*
simple. *Englishers* go out of their way to buy Amish-
made products, so I think you should consider having
Amish in the name. It will help you sell more products
with no extra effort."

"All right."

"And your first name?"

"Wouldn't that be prideful?"

"Well, you'll want something to distinguish your
ironwork from other Amish's. Think about it while we
get the rest of it set up."

In the end, he chose *Rainbow Amish Ironworks*.

It gave her a swirl of pleasure inside that he put part
of the name he'd given her in the title even if he didn't
realize it. She wasn't about to connect those dots for
him. He might change his mind.

"I feel as though *meine* head's been run over by a
plow."

She laughed out loud. "I imagine it does." She
walked him outside.

"Thank you for doing all that computer stuff for
me."

"Thank you for building me half of a *haus*."

"Don't thank me yet. We're only half-finished." He
hitched up his buggy and drove away.

She leaned against one of the porch's support
posts and watched him leave. Why did Eli have to be
Amish? Why couldn't he have decided to leave like she
did? Why did he have to be so nice? All her questions

were answered in her first question. He was Amish through and through. The qualities he maintained by being Amish were the same ones that made him so attractive—kind, generous, hardworking—but also made him unattainable.

Chapter Ten

Early Thursday morning, Dori strolled along the shoulder of the road. *Grossvater* had set up an appointment with Dr. Kathleen. She didn't know what to expect from the doctor. Having been healthy as a child, she'd seen an *English* doctor only a few times when very young and a couple of times while she lived in the *Englisher* world. Though she liked the idea of an Amish doctor, she also found it a little unnerving. What would Kathleen Yoder be like now? Would she too be more *English* than Amish? When Kathleen had left, it was for a *gut* cause. Dori had left because she didn't want to stay. Didn't want to follow the rules. Would the doctor judge her for her choices? Chastise her for being pregnant and not married?

About a half of a mile into her trek, Eli approached in a two-wheeled trap from the direction she was headed. He pulled to the shoulder. "Where are you off to?"

The baby kicked at the sound of his voice.

"Dr. Kathleen's. *Meine grossvater* thinks I should have the baby checked to see how it's doing."

"And you're going on foot all that way?"

Dori hadn't wanted to, but there wasn't a horse and buggy available to her today. "*Ja.* I don't mind the walk."

"It's too far. I'll give you a ride." He jumped down and looked both ways. "It's safe to cross." He waved her over.

Like she couldn't figure that out for herself. She wouldn't say anything though. She appreciated his thoughtfulness and the ride. As well as the time she would get to spend with him.

He met her in the middle of the two-lane road.

How nice of him to be protective—something Craig had never been—but she could check for traffic and cross a street by herself.

He helped her up and climbed in himself.

The baby squirmed to one side of her belly, as though trying to get closer to Eli.

Once they were at the clinic, he tethered the horse.

"You don't have to come in or stay. I'll have enough energy to walk home since I didn't have to walk here. I don't want to keep you from your work."

"You'll need a ride home. I'll stay." He opened the door and went inside with her.

She doubted any amount of arguing would change his mind, and she would not only appreciate another ride but his company, as well.

Jessica Yoder checked Dori's name off a short list on a pad of paper. Was that the extent of the clinic's check-in procedure? "I'll tell the doctor you're here." She went to the back.

With no one else in the waiting area, Dori sat on the love seat and Eli in a padded armchair.

Dr. Kathleen came out quickly. "Dorcas Bontrager?"

Dori stood. "Call me Dori."

The doctor nodded. "Come on back." She motioned toward an open door, then she spoke to Eli. "Will you be waiting for her?"

"Ja."

"Noah's in his workshop in the barn. You'll probably be happier out there."

"Danki, I would like that." Eli left.

Dori stared at the exam table. No paper covered it. Instead, an actual cloth sheet lay over the flat surface.

When she hesitated, the doctor spoke. "Don't worry. We put on a fresh sheet for each patient."

Dori hopped up and let her legs dangle over the edge.

Dr. Kathleen asked a series of questions about her medical history. The doctor wasn't what Dori had expected. She seemed very Amish, yet she had a medical degree.

As Dori gave her answers, she noted that the doctor wrote everything on paper. "Wouldn't it be faster to put your notes directly into a computer?"

"I wish." The doctor pointed her pen around the room. "All *meine* records here are paper files."

"That must be a pain. You haven't been approved to have a computer." That was wrong. Of anyone, the doctor should have a computer. She would talk to *Grossvater*.

"I have a computer I use for research and communicating with other doctors, but that's it."

"What about your own website?"

"I don't need a website."

"I disagree. *Englisher* doctors can find you and recommend you to their Amish patients."

"I don't want to take anyone's patients."

Sometimes the Amish were too nice for their own *gut*. "You should at least have a patient database. It would make your life as a doctor easier."

"I know. We used them in medical school and hospitals. I'm not as *gut* with a computer as I am with people."

"I can build one for you."

"Really?"

Dori had learned quite a bit from Craig, classes at the public library and various places online. In the *English* world, she felt as though she knew next to nothing about computers, but here, in the Amish community, her knowledge vastly exceeded anyone's.

Eli bade Noah Lambright farewell. He couldn't imagine what was taking Rainbow Girl so long. Had the doctor found something wrong? He hurried inside the clinic.

No one sat in the waiting area. Jessica wasn't at her reception desk. Female voices came from one of the back rooms.

"Hallo?" He leaned to the side to peer toward the voices.

"Come on back," one of them called.

He stepped to the doorway of the doctor's office.

Four women sat in chairs huddled around a laptop: the doctor, Rainbow Girl, Jessica and Deborah Miller.

Jessica glanced up with a smile. "Dori's teaching us how to use the computer. She's going to create a patient database for us. And she's showing Deborah how to search for natural remedies. It's amazing how much information is in one small machine."

Rainbow Girl raised her gaze. "The information isn't *in* the computer. It's out there—" she waved her hand carelessly "—in cyberspace. The computer merely finds it for you."

Deborah shook her head. "I still don't understand how information can be out *there* but not really *be* anywhere. It helps me to think of it in a building like a library. Dori has saved us a lot of time."

Saved Eli a lot of time, as well. Because of Rainbow Girl, his business would get a running start far sooner than he could have imagined. She already had the knowledge he had hoped to gain this summer. And she wouldn't be making all the mistakes he inevitably would. Trial and error. Trial and error. That was how he'd honed his smithing skills.

He wished she would decide to stay. If she could see how much he needed her, maybe she would.

Late Saturday afternoon, Dori stood in the middle of her new bedroom. It smelled fresh and clean.

Having spent Thursday afternoon and all day Friday with Daniel and Benjamin covering the inside with drywall and the exterior with siding, Eli worked alone today to put the finishing touches on the addition. He knelt to attach the final electric outlet cover and stood. "All done."

How could one man have so much kindness in him? He never criticized her for her poor choices and worked without complaint for a person he had to feel was undeserving. *"Danki."*

"*Bitte.* I have a couple of things outside. I'll be right back." He trotted out.

She turned to *Grossvater*, who stood with her. "And *danki* to you too." No one had done anything this nice for her since before she left the Amish community. "I don't know what I would have done without your help."

"'One should not abandon one's own; *Gott* does not abandon His own.'" *Grossvater* liked the German proverbs. There seemed to always be one to fit most any situation.

She walked around the bigger of the two bedrooms, never having had her own before. She'd shared with her sister growing up, then with Craig, then the homeless shelter and lastly *Grossvater*'s living room. Technically, these rooms belonged to *Grossvater*, but they were hers to freely use. She blinked away the excessive water in her eyes. This was nothing to cry over. "Now all I need are a few pieces of furniture, but I'm happy to sleep on the floor to have *meine* own space."

"Ah. Just wait." *Grossvater*'s eyes twinkled like a little boy's.

"For what?"

Voices drifted in through the back door. She peered out of her room to the parade of family members tromping into the *dawdy haus* along with Eli. No one came empty-handed. The only person missing was her oldest brother, Matthew.

Her bed from the big *haus*. A small dresser, a nightstand, sheets, quilts, a floor rug, curtains, as well as the family crib last used when ten-year-old John was a baby. Eli nailed a wrought iron clothing rack with five hooks on it to the wall. He hung a three-hook rack over the door. In a matter of a half an hour, her room, as well as the baby's, was furnished and ready to be occupied.

The tears Dori had held at bay earlier welled up in her eyes now. She didn't deserve any of this.

Mutter sidled up next to her. "I'm so pleased you've come home."

Dori smiled. "This is only temporary."

Vater spoke. "Supper's almost ready in the big *haus*. Everyone, wash up and come inside." His gaze skimmed over Dori as he said *everyone.* "You too, Eli. You've earned it."

Vater was including her in the invitation. She touched his sleeve. "*Danki* for all this."

He didn't look at her but kept his focus straight ahead. "*Bitte.* See to it you haven't put your *grossvater* and the whole family through all of this for nothing." He walked away.

But that was exactly what she planned. She couldn't stay here forever. This could be nothing but temporary.

Her family filed out, but Eli lingered. "Tell me this hasn't been a waste of time."

She knew he wanted her to tell him she was staying, but she couldn't. She wouldn't lie to him. "It's not a waste of anything. I do need a place to live."

"But you still don't plan to stay, do you?"

Unable to bear his scrutiny, she shifted her gaze to the blue-and-red braided rug on the floor.

His boots clunked on the wood floor as he walked away from her.

The following Tuesday, Eli pulled up in his wagon to the bishop's *dawdy haus* to find three buggies out front. Who was visiting him? He parked, set the brake and jumped down. He tethered Dutch and went up to the open door.

Rainbow Girl sat at the table with five people gathered around her, four men standing and a woman sitting in the chair next to her. "I have enough information here. I can create a mock website by tomorrow for you to preview."

Eli stepped inside. "What's going on?"

Rainbow Girl smiled, sending his insides dancing. "I'm helping them with their computers and websites."

"Does the bishop know about this?"

"Of course. Since I was helping him check on everyone's websites, I figured I could do a little work to keep their computers running well and fine-tune their sites."

Each of the people thanked her, then bade her farewell.

She crossed to the kitchen. "Would you like a glass of water?"

"*Ja*, I am thirsty."

She filled two glasses, gave him one and drank half of hers. "I was supposed to go over to your forge today to take pictures of your ironworks for the website. But time got away from me helping all these other people. I'm sorry."

"Not to worry. I brought the pieces to you. They are in *meine* wagon." He followed her outside.

Metal pieces jutted every which way above the edge of the wagon bed. He swung his arm toward his handiwork. "*Meine* inventory."

"You didn't have to do that. This had to be a lot of work, not to mention taking it all back and unpacking it."

He'd been glad to do it to save her some effort. "I

thought it would be easier if I brought them to you."
Easier for her, but definitely not for him.

"Well, *danki*, but you didn't have to go to all this
trouble." She peeked over the side of the wagon bed.
"Is this *everything* you've made?"

"*Ja*. I didn't know if I would need a different inventory number for each item since no two are identical."

"Well, you could give each piece a unique identify-
ing number. Or you could give an inventory number to
a type of item with a disclaimer that because these are
all handmade, the item received might differ from the
item pictured. The second option would be less work
for you." Or at least in the beginning, less work for her
until he took over the site.

"I know it's more work, but I like the idea of customers being able to choose the exact item they wish
to purchase. No disappointments. Which way do you
think would be best?"

"Either way would be fine. However, if you number
each item individually, I wouldn't recommend putting
more than six of a single type of item on the website.
Too many choices will overwhelm your customers and
might discourage them from clicking that purchase
button."

He was the one overwhelmed. Too much to do. Too
much to contemplate. Too many decisions. But Rainbow Girl seemed to take this all in stride and knew
what needed to be done. "Would you consider helping me with *meine* website a couple of times a week?"

"A *couple*?"

He'd asked too much. "Or just once. Until I get the
hang of things." He really needed her help. She'd prob-

ably thought that once she'd created his website, she would be done.

She shifted to face him. "You will have regular orders. We should work on them at least three times a week. You don't want people to cancel because their merchandise isn't processed quickly enough."

At least three times? He liked the sound of that. "I could do that. Mondays, Wednesdays and Fridays? I'll come here."

"That sounds *gut*, but not here. I should go to your forge. That's where all your inventory is." Her gaze skimmed over his wagon, and she smiled. "Usually."

"But after everything is numbered and tagged, I would need to bring only new items." He didn't want her trying to walk to his place three days a week. Plus, if she got busy like today, he would be assured of seeing her. "So it's settled. I'll come here." He wanted that little bit of control, and to not have to stand around waiting and wondering when she would arrive.

"Won't that cut into your work time? You won't be able to make as many pieces."

But he'd be with her. That would be time well spent. "I'll have plenty of time to work."

"You are as stubborn as *Grossvater*."

"Danki." Now, if he could be more stubborn than her about whether she stayed or not.

The next afternoon, Dori relaxed on the front porch of the *dawdy haus* in a rocking chair, grateful to be done staring at the computer screen for a while.

Ruth brought out two glasses of lemonade and sat, as well.

Dori took a long drink. "That hits the spot."

Ruth too took a swallow and licked her lips. "Mmm. I'm glad for summer break."

"That doesn't sound very Amish. I thought all Amish were supposed to love hard work."

"I do love teaching, but I'm as anxious as the children for the school year to end. Tell me about Eli."

Dori's mouth threatened to smile at the mention of his name. "You know who Eli is. He's a blacksmith."

"*Ne.* Tell me about *you* and Eli."

She wished. "There is no *me* and Eli."

Ruth shook her head. "I see the looks between you two. He likes you."

"You are seeing things."

"He built you half of a *haus.*" Ruth pointed behind her.

"Because our *grossvater* asked him to. One doesn't say *ne* to the bishop."

"The addition is completed, and still he comes over here. Wasn't he here yesterday? And the day before?"

"I'm helping him with his website and to get the word out online about his business."

"You don't give anyone else in the community as much attention as you give him, or he gives you." Ruth wiggled her eyebrows.

Dori huffed a breath. "Give it a rest, sister."

"Not until you admit you like him back."

"I will admit no such thing. And even if I had any feelings—however small—it wouldn't matter because I'm leaving after the baby is born."

Her sister leaned forward in her chair. "Dori, you can't. You have to stay. You're the only sister I have. Who will I talk to about Daniel?"

"You have plenty of cousins and other women in the community."

Mutter appeared on the porch with a covered plastic bowl, three smaller bowls and forks. "I cut up some fresh fruit. It'll be *gut* for the baby."

"Are you supposed to be here? Won't *Vater* get upset?"

"Since you started the classes to join church, he doesn't mind. I'm so happy you're going to stay."

Would it do any *gut* to contradict her? But she just couldn't let her *mutter* be misled. "*Mutter*, I'm not planning to stay."

Mutter dished them each up a bowlful. "Your *grossvater* had a room built for you."

"Against *meine* wishes." Dori was so grateful for her own space. "It seems no one in this community will believe me when I say I'm not staying." She took a bite of a juicy red strawberry. Sweet and delicious. "Mmm." She took piece after piece as though she were a starving child. She wasn't, of course. She was just pregnant and perpetually hungry.

As Dori popped her last grape into her mouth, Eli drove up in an open two-wheeled trap.

Ruth pointed. "See what I mean?"

Mutter perked up. "Is there something going on between those two?"

Dori spoke before her sister could. "*Ne.*" She jumped to her feet and met Eli under the shade of the tree.

He stopped but didn't get out. "I wanted to talk to you about a couple of new items for *meine* website, but I can see that you're busy. I'll come back another time."

Mutter stepped off the porch. "Eli Hochstetler, it's

so *gut* to see you. I was talking to your *mutter* after church on Sunday."

He nodded to her. "I don't want to interrupt."

"You aren't interrupting. Is he, Dorcas? Come and join us. Have some fresh fruit." She waved him down. "I won't take *ne* for an answer."

Dori's *mutter* wasn't being very subtle. Had she and her sister planned this? Were they ganging up on her? It wouldn't do any *gut*. Dori wasn't going to change her mind about staying, but no one seemed to want to listen to her. She could no more be Amish than Craig could.

Without further refusal, Eli set the brake and joined them on the porch.

Mutter remained standing. "I have some cookies I baked yesterday. I'll run to the big *haus* and get them." She returned faster than Dori thought possible. Had she actually *run*? Evidently she really wanted Eli to stay.

Dori wasn't going stop her. She liked having Eli around too, but nothing was going to develop between them. Nothing could. Eli saw her as an *Englisher*, and Dori was planning to return to the *Englisher* world as soon as she could. In the meantime, she would enjoy his company. "What are the items you have in mind to add to your inventory?"

He trotted to his buggy and returned with a twelve-inch-tall twisted piece of metal and a short one with two sides. They each had leaves decorating them. "What do you think?"

She studied them a moment and took the taller one. "Paper towel holder, and that one's for napkins." She pointed to the one he still held.

"Right. Do you think people will want to buy these?"

"Of course they will. Maybe even buy them as a set. These are beautiful."

"You can keep those."

Oh, dear. He was giving her gifts now. That couldn't be *gut.* "*Ne.* I don't have a kitchen, but I'll take pictures and upload them to your website." He needed to keep his inventory to sell, and these would definitely fetch a fine price.

"I can make more."

"I appreciate the offer, but you need to keep them." When his countenance faltered, she quickly added, "For now. You're making some regular sales, but you need to keep the momentum going and have constant marketing to make your business thrive. Having a new product like these will help."

"But I want to give back for all the work you're doing for me."

"Have you forgotten about the half of a *haus* you built?" Why didn't he realized the enormity of that? Far more than a little website.

Ruth gave a conspicuous nod to *Mutter.*

As long as neither of them said anything embarrassing, Dori could ignore them.

The pair of them behaved. For the most part. They fawned over him like one might a TV celebrity, asking him questions and being overly interested in his blacksmithing. But it worked for Dori, because she learned much about the humble man Eli had grown into, yet she remained the innocent bystander.

After services on Church Sunday, Ruth hooked her arm around Dori's. "I have a favor to ask you, sister."

Dori sighed. "When you say it like that, I sense I'm not going to like it."

"As you noticed, I'm partial to Daniel Burkholder. Would you ask Eli to have him and Daniel ask *Vater* if they can take you and I for a buggy ride?"

That was a lot of asking and a roundabout way of doing things. But it was the Amish way. It wasn't a *gut* idea for Dori to go on a buggy ride with Eli. She already spent too much time with him, bringing her closer to him. People in the community were likely talking about them. That couldn't be *gut* for Eli. "I can ask Eli to ask Daniel to ask you on a buggy ride."

"You must come too. *Vater* won't let me go alone with a young man. You know how he is."

Ja. When Dori was a teen, she'd sneaked out several times to meet a boy. Usually for a simple walk or to go fishing at a pond. Until she'd left the community. She supposed that sneaking off had led to taking more and more chances until she left altogether. And her leaving probably led to *Vater* being more strict with Ruth. "*Ja*, I'll ask."

"Right now?"

"They're playing horseshoes. I'll wait until he's done."

Her sister's expression turned worried.

Dori had missed her sister. "Fine. I'll ask now."

Ruth beamed. *"Danki."*

Dori nodded as she walked away. She approached Eli near the barn with several other young men, including Daniel. She waited until he threw his last horseshoe. "Eli?"

"Continue without me." Eli strode over to her.

The other men nodded and smiled as though they

knew a secret. A secret about her and Eli. They were wrong, of course.

He had that expression that came right before a smile. An expectation. An understated pleasure.

She soaked it in.

"Guten tag." His smile nearly undid her.

She glanced over his shoulder to regain her focus. "I have a favor to ask of you, but don't read anything into *meine* request."

"All right." His smile dipped below the surface again and lurked, waiting to be released again.

"Meine sister wants you and Daniel to ask our *vater* if you can take us on a buggy ride. Ruth is sweet on Daniel."

"I'd be happy to."

Dori was surprised. That hadn't taken any convincing at all. "Do you think Daniel will agree?"

"Ja. He's sweet on her, as well. We'll ask your *vater*, then come over to where you and your sister are."

"Danki." She walked back to Ruth, who looked giddy with excitement.

"Well?"

"They are going to ask *Vater*."

Across the Burkholders' yard, Eli and Daniel stood with *Vater*, who shook his head. The conversation volleyed between them several times. It looked as though Eli was trying to convince *Vater* to let them all go. Finally, *Vater* nodded, and Eli and Daniel headed toward her and her sister.

Dori touched Ruth's arm. "Don't appear too excited. Make him work a little for your affections."

Eli spoke. "I'm afraid we won't be able to take you ladies for a buggy ride today."

Ruth's shoulders slumped.

Daniel spoke. "Since church is at our home, I can't leave. I must stay in case I'm needed, but your *vater* has agreed to let us take you both to the fireworks in a week and a half if you want to—"

"*Ja,*" Ruth chirped.

So much for making him work a little for her affections. Dori stared up at Eli and hesitated a moment longer before answering. "*Ja*. I'd like that too." Her insides did a giddy little dance.

The hint of a smile played at the corners of his mouth.

Chapter Eleven

The following Saturday, Dori pulled on her voluminous gray split-skirt pants. She had outgrown her other clothes in a hurry, even her sweatpants and yoga pants. Eating well was doing both her and her baby well. The stretchy T-shirt knit was the only thing she could still get over her ever-growing belly. She hated these pants almost as much as cape dresses. She didn't know why she had even bothered to pack them when she left, but she was glad she had.

Dori had spent much of the past two weeks evaluating and updating Amish websites, teaching a recalcitrant bishop to use a computer, running virus scans and cleaning up hard drives for community members. No one seemed to understand that these things needed to be done regularly. *Grossvater* was nearly as uncooperative as Eli to learn. All of which had left her little time to create the doctor's database or study for the GED.

Now she was off to Dr. Kathleen's to transfer the database she'd built for her. She'd made it according to the doctor's specifications, and now she needed to install it on the computer at the clinic. "*Grossvater?* May I use your buggy?"

"Are you going to visit Eli?"

"*Ne.*" Though she wouldn't mind seeing him. It was harder to run into him with the addition finished. Fortunately, the arrangement to meet three days a week to update his site and fill orders gave her some regular interaction. "I'm going to the medical clinic."

"But you just saw Kathleen a couple of weeks ago. Is something wrong?"

"*Ne.* I'm not going for a medical visit. I'm installing the database I made for her and see if she likes how it works. There might be other things she may have realized she needs for it to work well for her. These kinds of things are usually a work in progress."

"You know a lot about computers and such."

She supposed she did. She hadn't realized how much she'd learned from Craig. "It's a skill I believe more and more Amish are going to need to learn in this day and age if their businesses are going to survive."

"I don't like all this technology—not one bit—but I suppose you're right. The world is a different place from when I was a boy. We don't have the advantage of isolating ourselves any longer. We are being pulled ever faster into the *Englisher* world."

"We were never truly isolated. The Amish have always been dependent on the *English* to purchase our produce and goods." She cocked her head. "Why are you smiling?"

"You said *we.* '*We* were never truly isolated.' You are still Amish at heart."

Ne, she wasn't. "Don't read anything into that. So

may I use your buggy? I would use *Vater*'s open two-wheeled buggy, but it looks like it might rain."

"*Ja*, for sure it will rain. I don't need *meine* buggy today. I'll have one of the boys hitch it up for you."

"*Danki.*" She went to the bathroom and pulled out her makeup bag. She'd taken to applying her makeup with a lighter touch these days. But as she started today, she halted. Why should she even bother wasting her makeup on people who didn't care about it? Correction, they did care and preferred she didn't wear it at all. So she dropped her eye shadow back into her bag. She would save it for when she returned to the *English* world, to people who cared about such things.

Instead, she experimented with twisting her hair away from her face. When she did so, her brown roots were almost long enough to hide the various colors on the side of her head where her hair hung longer. She tucked in a few bobby pins and attempted the same on the other side. Not nearly as successful. The shorter hair poked out in red spikes all along the roll she'd made, but she stuck in a few bobby pins anyway. Then she twisted the back of her hair and secured it to her head with the remainder of the bobby pins.

She chuckled. She almost looked Amish again. Plain and ugly. She yanked the pins out and shook her hair free. That was better. She may be without makeup and her facial piercings, but she wouldn't give up her fun, colorful hair or her multiple earrings.

After grabbing her backpack with her laptop, she headed out for the barn. Though dark clouds crowded the morning sky, no rain fell yet, but she could feel it coming.

In the barn, her brother Matthew attached the buggy poles to Nelly's harness.

She hadn't seen much of her oldest brother since she'd returned. "*Danki* for hitching the buggy for me."

Finishing, he glared at her and strode away without a word.

"Matthew? Stop."

He halted but didn't turn around.

She watched his shoulders rise slowly and fall as he drew in a long, slow, deep breath. She walked over and around in front of him. "Is something wrong?"

He narrowed his eyes and glowered at her. "Wrong? *You* are what's wrong. I stayed here. I've worked hard for *Vater*. What did you do? You ran off to the *English* world and returned pregnant. You don't deserve to be here. You don't belong here. You left. You're not Amish. And you never will be. Go back to where you came from." He stormed off.

Her brother hated her. A pain twisted in her chest.

She knew her family and friends would likely shun her—but since she hadn't joined church, they hadn't. She never expected anyone to outright hate her. Not like that. Matthew clearly did. That hurt more than she would have expected.

She ached to cry out to *Gott* as she'd done as a child when someone hurt her feelings, but she hadn't spoken to Him in a very long time. He wouldn't be interested in her pain, not after she'd turned her back on Him and her—the Amish people.

She longed to go after her brother and say something to make him not hate her, but everything he'd said was true. She *had* left. She *was* pregnant. And she *didn't* belong.

The problem was, she didn't feel like she belonged anywhere. Not here with the Amish, and not with the *Englishers* either. Oh, she'd faked it while she was out in the world, she'd dressed and played the part, but never truly felt *English*. Now she looked like a confused mess. Not Amish, and not *English*. What was she doing? She should leave, but where would she go? She had no place. As long as she was pregnant, Craig didn't want her. Or their baby. She couldn't return to the shelter. She couldn't live on the streets. Unfortunately, this was the only place that would have her.

She was the prodigal child, and her brother the *gut* child who had stayed behind.

She walked Nelly out of the barn, climbed into the buggy and drove away. By the time she arrived at Dr. Kathleen's, a sprinkling rain tapped lightly on the roof.

Noah Lambright met her outside the clinic. "Go on inside. I'll take care of your horse and buggy."

"Danki." She grabbed her pack and ran for the cover of the porch and knocked on the door.

After a moment, Dr. Kathleen opened the door. "You don't have to knock. When it's unlocked, I'm here and you can simply walk in."

Dori stepped inside. "I wasn't sure, since you aren't normally open on Saturdays."

The doctor closed the door. "I knew you were coming. Deborah Miller is also here doing some research for her *mutter.*"

That surprised Dori. "She's allowed to do that?"

"Ja. Her *mutter* has Graves' disease. She's been successful at finding natural remedies that seem to be helping. Her *mutter* is also pregnant and due about the same time as you."

"Really? She's not too old?"

"*Ne.* Her body is still healthy despite her condition."

That shouldn't surprise Dori that an older Amish woman would be pregnant. Amish women had plenty of babies in their later years. *Englishers* would be far more upset at a later-in-life child after having raised a family. "I've finished the database. Sorry to have taken so long."

"Not to worry. I've been without it this long, I'm just excited to have it now."

A very different attitude from the hurry-up *English.* Dori would have been fired by now. "I want you to look at it and see if there are any other features you'd like me to add." She lifted her backpack. "I have a laptop in here." It was *Grossvater*'s new one, but he wasn't about to use it or even open it without Dori twisting his arm.

Dr. Kathleen indicated the table that served as the reception desk. "Deborah's using *meine* computer in the office, so we can look at it out here."

Jessica, the doctor's sister, stood and moved behind the chair. "Do you mind if I watch?"

"Not at all. It sounded like you will be working with the database as much as the doctor." Dori set down her laptop and lifted the lid. While she waited for it to boot up, she took out her cell phone. Still no call or text from Craig, but he hadn't cut off her service. That said something. She set the phone aside, opened the database program from the thumb drive and offered Dr. Kathleen the chair. "I put in a few phantom patient records so you'd have something to look at and click from one record to another." She instructed the doctor about the features.

Dr. Kathleen clicked around for a few minutes. "You

did a great job. This is just what I need. How do we get it onto *meine* computer?"

Dori tapped the red thumb drive sticking out from the side of her laptop. "It's all on here. I just need to plug this into yours, and it'll transfer quickly."

The doctor stood. "Great. Let Jessica use it for a few minutes to scc if she thinks of anything to be added. I'll go check to see how much longer Deborah will be."

Though hesitant at first, Jessica warmed up fast to the program.

"I think you're a natural."

"I'm trying to learn about computers. I want to get *meine* GED and take business classes on the computer to get a degree."

Dori perked up. "I'm working on *meine* GED too."

"Would you like to work on our GEDs together? I don't really know what I'm doing."

"I would like that. It will help me, as well."

They arranged for Jessica to come to the bishop's *haus* two days a week so they could study together.

Dr. Kathleen came back out. "She's almost done, so we can move in there and be ready when she is."

With her computer in hand, Dori followed Jessica and the doctor into her office.

Dr. Kathleen indicated the girl behind the desk. "You know Deborah."

"I'm almost done. Let me write down a few of these website addresses. I wish they weren't so long and confusing." Deborah scratched one long convoluted number and letter combination under her previous one.

"There's an easier way to do that." Dori showed her how to bookmark web pages.

"*Danki!* That's so much easier." Deborah added several more.

Why couldn't Eli be as eager to learn this stuff and try on his own? But then, if he did, she wouldn't get to spend nearly as much time with him.

These three women were unique for the Amish. All would increase their computer knowledge before Dori left. She would see to it. It would be her legacy.

Deborah stood. "All done thanks to Dori. *Danki*, Dr. Kathleen. I found some interesting information that I hope helps. I'm going to hurry home before the rain really starts coming down. *Auf Wiedersehen.*" Deborah dashed out.

Dori sat behind the desk and plugged in the thumb drive. "You know what this means, don't you?"

Dr. Kathleen took a seat across from the desk. "That I'll be able to organize *meine* patients' files and search them more easily?"

"Besides that. You'll need another computer for Jessica at your front desk."

Jessica beamed.

The doctor held up her hand to her sister. "Don't get too excited. That's not likely to happen. The church leaders were reluctant to approve one. I doubt they'll approve two." Dr. Kathleen stood abruptly. "I'll be back." She ran from the room and into the bathroom.

Dori turned to Jessica. "Is she all right?"

"Morning sickness. She's finally pregnant."

When the doctor returned, she seemed fine, though a bit pale-faced.

"I hear congratulations are in order."

She smiled. "*Danki.* It appears our dear Lord has chosen to bless me with a child after all."

"I'm so happy for you."

"When it hadn't happened right away, people whispered that I was being punished for staying away for so long and becoming a doctor."

Dori frowned. "Do you believe that? That *Gott* was punishing you?"

"*Ne.* I don't believe *Gott* does that. He's a *gut* and kind and loving *Gott*. He waited for His right time. Like sending you back to us. All in *Gott*'s timing."

Dori didn't believe that. The timing had been terrible. She'd lost everything and had nowhere to live. But then, the Amish would say that it had been exactly the right timing.

By the time Dori was ready to leave, the rain fell harder. It ebbed and flowed. Soft, then hard, then soft again.

"Do you want to wait until this lets up?" Dr. Kathleen stood in the open doorway.

Dori looked toward the dark sky. "I don't think it's going to completely let up anytime soon. Maybe not even today at all. I should leave now before it gets any worse. I'll be fine."

"All right." The doctor pulled the short rope of the bell that hung from the porch awning, and a clang rang out.

Her husband appeared in the barn doorway.

Dr. Kathleen pointed to Dori. "Buggy!"

He nodded and disappeared. A few minutes later, he reemerged, holding an umbrella and leading Dori's horse.

Dori dashed from the porch through the open buggy door. *"Danki."* She drove away.

As Nelly trotted down the road, Dori turned her

mind to Eli. Next week, she should go over to his place and take pictures of his work environment to add a bit of depth to the site. Tell the story of how some of the different pieces were made.

Pictures?

Her phone. She didn't remember putting it in her pack.

With one hand holding the reins, she used her other to check the pack's pocket where she normally kept her phone. Nothing. She checked the other pockets. Not there either, so she unzipped her pack and felt around the interior. *Where was it?* She tucked the reins under her arm to hold them while she dug with both hands. No phone.

A car honked.

Dori jerked her attention back to driving. Nelly had wandered into the middle of the two-lane country road. Dori pulled the reins to the side, and the horse moved into her lane again.

Still honking, the car sped up and passed. The boys inside yelled and hooted as they flew by with their music blaring through the open windows. Road water splashed up on the horse as well as the buggy.

Nelly hopped on her forelegs a couple of times and bolted.

The reins pulled out from under Dori's arm. She grappled for the leather strips and managed to grab hold of them. "Whoa!"

Nelly fought the reins at first but then slowed, settling into her previous leisurely walk.

Dori's heart pounded. Didn't motorists know to be cautious when passing an animal? Evidently, teenagers didn't. Probably thought it amusing to spook a horse. As well as its driver.

Nelly favored one of her front hooves.

Dori maneuvered the horse to the shoulder and hauled back on the reins. After setting the brake, she stepped out into the steady but now light rain. She stroked the side of the big draft horse's neck. "Shh. It's all right."

Nelly's hide quivered, and she swung her head toward Dori.

She stroked the leg in question and raised the hoof. The shoe had been thrown.

As a pickup approached from the opposite direction, Nelly nickered, retrieved her leg and pawed the ground. Though the vehicle traveled at a normal speed, the horse was still unnerved.

"It's all right, girl." Dori gripped the harness leather behind the horse's jaw.

The truck slowed a bit as it passed, as though trying to reduce the amount of road splash.

Nelly wasn't having any of it. She tried to rear, but Dori held tight. She needed to keep the horse from getting any more agitated. Nelly jerked her head to free herself.

"*Ne.* Calm down." Life was so much easier with a car. A car didn't get spooked and need to be soothed.

The horse swung her head toward Dori, knocking her off balance. If not for her grip on the harness, Dori would have fallen. Then Nelly wrenched her head the other way, jerking the harness from Dori's grip. She reared and, apparently realizing she was free, lurched forward with the buggy and galloped into a run.

The rear wheel clipped Dori's hip and spun her half-way around.

She lost her footing and slid down the muddy embankment on her backside, causing her wide-legged pants to travel up. At the bottom and in two-foot-high weeds, her ankle hit something hard. A sharp pain shot up her leg. Had she hit a rock or a branch? Either way, it had banged her bone. Wiggling her foot, she assessed that no bones had been broken, but she likely had a cut, a scrape at the very least. As she reached down to feel her ankle, she also straightened her sodden pant legs. She couldn't tell, with all the mud and rain, if there was blood on her ankle, as well.

A wall of bushes and trees stood beyond the weeds. Forward wouldn't be a wise direction, so she rolled to her stomach and clawed her way up the steep embankment. Reaching the halfway point, she slid back down the muddy slope, hitting her other ankle this time but not as hard. Twice more, she made it halfway before slipping to the bottom again. Though pain shot through her first injured ankle, she *had* managed to climb with it, assuring her no bones had been broken but definitely injured.

The sound of a car coming down the road caught her attention.

She hollered and waved her arms, but the bank stood a little too tall for her to be seen.

The motorist drove right on by, completely unaware someone needed help.

Poor frightened Nelly. How far had she run? If the horse and buggy were close, a passerby would eventually stop to investigate. Hopefully sooner rather than later. If Nelly made it all the way home by herself, someone would realize something had gone wrong, but no one would know exactly where to look for Dori. She would just have to wait. Someone would eventually find her.

She turned her thoughts heavenward. Gott? *Please, help me get out of this mess.*

What was she praying to Him for? He hadn't listened to her prayers in the past. But it couldn't hurt, could it?

A moment later, the rain increased to a torrent.

With closed eyes, she tilted her head toward the sky. "Seriously!" Wasn't her life bad enough? She rolled to her back and leaned against the steep bank. At this point, she couldn't get any wetter, but the heavy rain would wash off some of the mud. She could at least be grateful for that.

She didn't know how long she leaned there with her ankle throbbing while the rain washed her face. A stream of water trickled over her feet.

How long before the heavy rain rose in the ditch, turning the stream into a rushing creek?

She wrapped her arms around her protruding belly. "Don't worry, baby, I'll protect you. *Gott*, please make the rain stop. And please, have someone come by and notice I'm here. Eli would be nice to send *meine* way."

But what were the chances he would happen to be out in the rain and happen to find her at the bottom of a ditch?

None.

Chapter Twelve

Eli swung his hammer down again and again on the red-hot piece of iron. This would be a rattle for Rainbow Girl's baby. He thought a lot about Rainbow Girl lately.

With the addition finished, he'd feared not seeing her, but he had been surprised she'd insisted upon working together on his business website and orders *three* days a week. He'd hoped for one day a week, tried for two, but she'd said they needed to meet *at least* three days a week or his online orders would suffer.

He was fortunate indeed. Her assistance allowed him to focus on making items to sell. He shook his head. He had to admit he'd been more focused on Rainbow Girl lately than his ironwork.

Eli dunked the rattle into his pail of water and set it aside to cool, then put out his forge fire. Though he usually liked working on cool, rainy days, and it wasn't one of his scheduled times, he wanted to see Rainbow Girl. Only to get her opinion on the marketability of his latest creation. Once she had taken photographs of it, he would give it to her as a gift. He also wanted to fine-tune some of his product descriptions and check on more orders. She kept trying to get him to buy a computer so he could manage all this himself, but he preferred to have her do it. Not only was that easier and gave him more time to create, but he got to spend time with her.

He hitched Dutch to a small open-air buggy with a cloth top. He didn't want to get drenched before he arrived, but he also didn't want to be closed in.

Once at the bishop's, he parked in front. He would wait until he knew if it would be all right to visit before unhitching Dutch and putting him in the barn. He bound up the steps and knocked.

Bishop Bontrager opened the door. "Eli, come in, come in."

Eli stepped inside. "I came to see Dorcas. About *meine* website." He didn't want the bishop to think there was anything more to his visit than that. Because there wasn't.

"She's not here. Went to Noah and Kathleen's to do something with a computer for the doctor." He glanced at the clock on the coffee maker. "I thought she would've returned by now. Said she wouldn't be gone long."

Eli's insides twisted. "Do you think she's all right?"

"I'm sure she is, but it wouldn't hurt to call. Our telephone's in the barn."

"I'll call. You stay here." Eli could move faster alone, and the old man didn't need to be out in the rain. He ran to the barn and found the community's typed directory in a wooden wall pocket by the phone. The doctor's number had been handwritten on the front. He dialed.

Noah answered.

"Dorcas Bontrager came to work on the doctor's computer. Is she still there?"

"*Ne*. She left a few hours ago. Is something wrong?"

Eli's insides wrenched harder into a painful knot. "I don't think so. Did she say if she planned to go anywhere from your place besides home?"

Noah made Eli wait while he asked the doctor. "*Ne*. Kathleen understood she was heading home. She left before the rain had gotten harder. Is she not there?"

"*Ne*. But I'm sure she's fine. She probably stopped to visit a neighbor. *Danki*." But Eli had a bad feeling. Rainbow Girl didn't socialize with others in the community except to work on their websites. Their people were still wary of her. Had she run away from the community again? Or had something happened to her? Either way, he needed to find her. He returned to the *dawdy haus*. "She's not there. She left hours ago. I'm going out to look for her."

The bishop headed out the door with him. "I'll send Andrew and Matthew in search of her as well, and have Leah call the neighbors."

Eli nodded as he climbed in his buggy. "I'll retrace the direct route between here and the doctor's. Have them check the alternate routes." He drove away at a faster clip than normal.

He arrived at the doctor's with no sight of her, here or on the road. Dr. Kathleen had been on the phone, calling neighbor after neighbor since he'd telephoned. No one knew Rainbow Girl's whereabouts.

That likely meant she'd gone to town since no one had seen her. Had she left them again? Left him. Though he wanted to go find her, he didn't want to know for sure that she'd left. He wanted to return to his forge and forget all about her. Pound the baby rattle into a lump. How would he figure out his website and manage his orders? He needed her. He would find her.

But when he pulled out onto the road, he headed back the way he'd come at a more normal pace this time. He didn't want to return without her, but he couldn't make himself head toward town and her face-to-face rejection.

About a third of the way, something in the road caught his attention. He stopped, got out in the rain and picked it up. A horseshoe. One he had fashioned. Had this come off Nelly? If so, Rainbow Girl had been heading home rather than into town. His spirits lifted, then crashed again. So where was she?

Shaking off the rain, he climbed back into his buggy and drove at a faster pace. Maybe she had arrived at the bishop's, and he'd somehow missed her.

About another mile down the road, he noticed a draft horse and buggy under some trees at the edge of a field. Not just any horse. Nelly. Maybe she had driven the horse there to wait out the storm. He hurried to the clump of trees. He jumped from his rig and opened the door of hers. Rainbow Girl wasn't inside, but her pack sat on the floor.

He scanned the vicinity. No Rainbow Girl. "Rainbow? Dori!" The nearest Amish *haus* wasn't even in sight. He knew which direction, but did she?

He lifted Nelly's front hoof that she held cocked. The shoe was missing. He unhitched the horse and secured her to a tree. "I'll return for you." He climbed aboard his buggy, intending to drive to the nearest *haus*. Instead, he headed back to where he'd found the horseshoe. He got out and looked up the road and down. Where would she have gone? Rain pelted him and ran off his hat. Was she out in this?

"Rainbow!" He listened. "Dori!" He didn't know what to call her.

If Nelly threw a shoe here and ended up a mile away, where had Rainbow Girl gone? He pulled the reins out in front of Dutch, turned him and walked down the side of the road.

She had been headed in this direction. Nelly's shoe had come off—for some reason. Something must have happened, because he'd checked her shoes not that long ago. One wouldn't have simply *fallen* off. Had she spooked?

"Rainbow! Dori!"

He heard a muffled voice and stopped the horse. "Rainbow?"

"I'm here."

The voice came from up ahead.

"Where?" He couldn't see her on either side of the road.

"The ditch."

He leaned over and saw her twenty-five yards up the road. He jogged, bringing the horse with him. Taking the tether weight from the floor of the buggy, he secured Dutch. It wouldn't do him any *gut* to have his horse wander off or spook and bolt.

"Are you all right? Are you hurt?"

Waterlogged and mud caked, she stood at the bottom of a ten-foot or so incline, staring up at him, with one hand on the muddy side of the embankment, the other on her stomach. "Wet and cold mostly. Other than that, I'm fine."

Was she really? Or merely telling him what he wanted to hear? "Is the baby all right?"

She sucked in a breath. "*Ja*. It's been kicking me. Gave me a real wallop at the sound of your voice."

That idea made him smile. Certainly the baby didn't know *his* voice, did it? "I'll get you two out of there." He moved closer to the edge.

She held up her hand. "What are you doing?"

"I'm coming down for you."

"*Ne!* It's too slippery to climb up. Why do you think I'm still down here? We don't want to both be stuck."

Just because she couldn't climb out, didn't mean he couldn't. "I can't reach you." Even prone on the ground, he doubted he could. Why hadn't he thought to bring a rope? Because he never imagined she'd be at the bottom of a deep ditch and he'd need one.

"Go get help."

Leave her? That didn't sit well with him. "I can't leave you down there."

"I'm not going anywhere. I promise to still be here when you return."

He would *not* abandon her. He would think of something else. "To your left a few feet, I can see a fallen tree branch. Do you think you can reach it?"

She looked. "I think so."

"Point one end of it up the bank for me to reach."

She turned and leaned for it, then sucked in a breath.

"What's wrong?" She wasn't going into labor, was she? She *was* a little over seven months pregnant. "Is it the baby?"

She shook her head. "I hurt *meine* ankle when I slid down here. I'll be fine." She grabbed a twig of the bigger branch and pulled the whole thing toward her.

Hopefully, it would be large enough and strong enough to use to pull her up. He needn't have worried. As she pulled the branch and maneuvered one end up the bank, it kept coming. Grunting and groaning, she eventually hoisted the thick end far enough for him to grab. "Let go of it." When she did, he pulled it all the way up.

"What about me? I thought you were going to hold it so I could climb up it."

"I am, but there are too many offshoots. I'm going to break off some of the smaller ones to make it easier to hold on to." Using his boot and leaning the branch against the buggy, he stomped off branch after branch but left a larger one near the base. He fed that end down the hill. "Put your arm between the larger branch and the one that shoots off from it."

"Why?"

"In case your hands slip, you won't fall." Her wet, muddy hands were small compared to his and not as strong. She also had to be tired from her ordeal.

"What if your hands slip?"

"They won't." He wouldn't let them. "Hold on and climb with your feet. I'll do most of the work."

She got into position as he'd instructed.

"*Gott*, please let her hold on tight and don't let the branch break." Hand over hand he hauled up the hunk of wood and Rainbow Girl along with it.

Halfway, her feet slipped from under her.

The branch slid a few inches in his grip, and he sucked in a breath. That definitely tore some flesh. "Are you all right?"

"*Ja.* Don't let go."

"I won't."

She got her feet back under her. "That seems to be the same place I kept slipping on *meine* own. You were right about having the offshoot under *meine* arm."

He'd been glad for it, as well. *Gott* had supplied what they needed. He hauled the branch up faster this time. He wanted to get her to safety as quickly as possible. When she was nearly at the top, his next reach latched onto her wrist, then her other wrist. He hefted her forward and into his arms. She was safe.

Her arms wrapped around him. "*Danki.* I didn't know how I was going to get out of there."

"You're safe." He searched her face to see if she was truly all right. He wiped rain and mud from it, then caressed her cheek.

As though some invisible force pushed him forward, he leaned closer. He pressed his lips to hers. Soft and sweet. Or had she kissed him? He couldn't tell. All he knew was he never wanted to let her go.

But he must and did. "Are you sure you're not hurt?"

"Only *meine* ankle." She held her foot out. A gash cut into her flesh.

He lifted her into his arms, and she sucked in a breath. "What is it?"

"*Meine* hip hurts too."

"What happened to your hip?"

"Nelly spooked and lost a shoe. I stopped to check her. When she bolted, the rear wheel clipped *meine* hip. It's only a bump. I'll be fine."

He leaned forward to set her in his buggy.

Her grip tightened around his neck, and her tone was alarmed. "What are you doing?"

"Setting you in the buggy."

"You can't. I'm all muddy."

"I'm aware of that." He was muddy now too from holding her. "I can easily clean the buggy. Now, let go of me so I can look at your injury." Not that he really wanted her to release him.

With a heavy sigh, she freed him.

He set her on the seat and assessed her ankle. "This doesn't look too deep, but it bled and is full of mud. I'm taking you back to the doctor."

"You don't have to do that. I can clean it and put a bandage on it when I get home. It'll be fine."

"This could get infected." He rounded the buggy and climbed in.

"It'll heal. We need to find Nelly."

"She's fine, which is more than I can say for you." He turned Dutch around and headed for the clinic.

"Think of the baby. Are you sure it's all right?"

"The baby's fine. Nelly threw a shoe somewhere around here. Maybe we can find it."

Amazing. She'd just been through a harrowing experience, and she was thinking of the horse. He pushed the horseshoe on the floor of the buggy with his boot. "Found it. That's why I was walking Dutch rather than driving, and the reason I could hear you when you called back to me."

"That was lucky."

"That was *Gott*."

During the whole drive, he could think of nothing but Rainbow Girl's well-being, the baby and...that kiss.

He shouldn't have done it but longed to do it again.

Dripping wet, Dori hooked her arms around Eli's neck as he carried her into the clinic. She didn't need him to carry her, but she liked being in his arms. She couldn't believe they'd kissed. It had sort of been a mutual meeting in the middle. Nice and sweet, but she knew he hadn't meant to do it. A *gut* Amish wouldn't kiss someone until they were at least engaged. Most didn't kiss until the wedding day.

Dr. Kathleen rushed over. "You found her. Bring her in here and set her on the table." She motioned toward one of the back rooms.

Dori swung her legs. "Don't you dare put me on that clean white sheet." She didn't want to get it all muddy. The black buggy seat had been bad enough.

"Would you stop worrying about a little dirt? You are more important than getting something dirty."

But someone would have to clean it up. "I can stand. Please let me."

The doctor gave him a nod, and he finally relented. "She has a cut on her ankle, and her hip's bruised. And make sure the baby's all right. She fell into a ditch."

Dori liked that he cared enough to not leave anything to chance.

Dr. Kathleen removed a washcloth and two towels from a chest of drawers. "I'll check her thoroughly. There are a lot of people out searching for her. Would you make a few calls and spread the message that she's been found and is well?"

He turned to leave but stopped at the doctor's voice. "In a lower cupboard in the kitchen are some extra towels to dry off with."

"*Danki*, Dr. Kathleen." Then he left.

The doctor set the towels on the dresser next to a plain white ceramic pitcher and basin. "I didn't think we needed him hovering. It's *gut* if he has something to do." She poured water from a pitcher into the basin.

"Your ankle seems to have stopped bleeding, so if you're all right to stand, you can wash up here. I'll get you something clean to wear."

Dori limped to where she could wash off some of the mud. Her thin knit pants, soggy and muddy, clung to her legs. *"Danki."*

The doctor opened a cabinet door behind Dori and closed it. "There are dry clothes on the table. If you're all right alone for a few moments, I'll retrieve more water. What you have will get dirty fast."

"I appreciate that. I'm fine." Once alone, she washed her face and hands, and did her best to get the mud from her arms.

Dr. Kathleen returned and swapped out a clean basin and pitcher and took away the dirty ones.

After washing up as best as she could, Dori removed her clothes and put them in a muddy pile near the door. She unfolded the clothes the doctor had left for her. A lavender cape dress. Of course. What else would an Amish woman have to offer? Dori didn't relish putting it on, but it was better than her filthy, sodden clothes. She never imagined wearing one of these again, but the dry dress felt *gut* against her cold, damp skin.

The doctor knocked on the door. "May I come in?" *"Ja."*

Dr. Kathleen entered with a smile. *"Wunderbar.* If you'll sit on the exam table, I'll see how you and the little one are doing."

Dori hopped up with her legs dangling over the edge. "I didn't actually *fall* into the ditch. I slid down the embankment on *meine* backside."

"Then the baby should be fine, but let's check to make sure." The doctor put her stethoscope on Dori's belly. "The heartbeat sounds strong." She pressed on various places on Dori's stomach. "Any pain?"

Dori shook her head.

After Dr. Kathleen seemed satisfied that the baby had escaped unscathed, she moved on to cleaning the cut on Dori's ankle and stitching it up. "Eli was very concerned about you."

She had noticed. "He seemed as relieved to have me out of the ditch as I was to be out. And he kept asking about the baby."

"I think he cares for you both."

"Not likely. The prodigal child and all, returning from the big, bad world. He needs me to manage his website. Nothing more." But that kiss did make her wonder.

"I think there's more than that."

"I'm not even planning to stay. He knows that, and *meine grossvater* knows that. Once the baby is born, I'm getting a job and finding an apartment."

"You could do worse than remaining with the Amish. Is it really so bad here?"

Dori knew that there were worse fates, but she didn't want this life. If Craig would take her back, she would be gone already. Never would have come.

After Dr. Kathleen finished examining and patching Dori up, they both went out into the reception area.

Eli's instant smile did funny things to Dori's insides that had nothing to do with the baby moving.

He shoved away from the counter he'd been leaning against. "How's the baby? Is it all right? It's not hurt, is it?"

The baby responded to his voice as it usually did. As it had when he'd pulled her out of the ditch.

The doctor gave Dori a knowing look. "The baby's fine, as is the *mutter*-to-be. The heartbeat is strong. From the bruising, the buggy hit only the outside of her hip, so no risk to the little one." She addressed Dori again. "I want to see you in a couple of days to check on your ankle, and also next week to remove the stitches. If you have any concerns, call anytime of the day or night."

Nodding, Dori limped to the reception desk. "I will. I think I left *meine* phone here." She picked it up from where she'd set it earlier. "If I'd had this, I could have called for help right away." But then, Eli might not have been the one to find her. And he never would have kissed her.

Dr. Kathleen handed Dori a pill bottle. "Take these for the pain."

Eli pointed at it. "Are those safe for the baby?"

The doctor shot Dori a quick, sideways glance. "I wouldn't give her anything that wasn't. She should rest for a few days and stay off her ankle as much as possible."

"I'll make sure she does." He scooped Dori up into his arms.

Dori caught her breath. "What are you doing?"

"Carrying you to the buggy."

"I can walk."

"The doctor said you're supposed to stay off your ankle."

The doctor opened the door for Eli. She was right about one thing. Eli really was worried about her and the baby, but that didn't mean he cared for her.

The rain had slowed to a drizzle.

He placed her gingerly into his buggy. "Are you comfortable?"

"Ja." How sweet of him to be so careful. "You cleaned the seat."

"I told you it would be all right."

Dr. Kathleen brought out a quilt. "Keep her warm."

The rain had put a chill in the air, and Dori's hair still hung in colorful wet tendrils.

With the quilt tucked around her, Eli drove off.

On the way, Dori spotted Nelly and pointed. "There she is."

"I'll return for her later."

"She's cold and wet and scared. Let's get her now."

Though he fussed and said the horse could wait, Eli guided the buggy off the road to where Nelly waited under the protection of the trees. He got out. "Wait here. I'll tie her to the back of *meine* buggy."

Once he had secured Nelly, Dori asked, "Would you get *meine* backpack with the computer in it, if it's even still there?"

Eli retrieved it without question.

Dori unzipped it. *Grossvater*'s laptop sat inside. She doubted she would be able to talk him into purchasing another one if it had been stolen.

Standing outside the buggy, Eli asked, "Anything else?"

"Ne."

With everything set, he climbed in again.

"Danki for searching for me and finding me." *And for that kiss*, she thought. Though it had likely just been a reaction to the situation, she would treasure it.

* * *

After supper, Eli worked in his forge. Two thoughts swam around and around in his head. Rainbow Girl could have been seriously hurt or died.

He also couldn't shake that kiss. He shouldn't have done that. The community frowned upon unmarried people kissing. But the feel of her lips on his had been wonderful. He wanted to kiss her again, but he couldn't. He wouldn't. He shouldn't.

Vater came around the corner and into the forge. "It's getting late."

Eli looked past his *vater* into the darkness. He must have been out here for hours for it to be so late. Where had the time gone? He certainly didn't have much to show for the time spent, a misshapen piece of iron and a dying fire. "I'll finish up here and be in shortly."

"You did well today in finding the bishop's *enkelin*. It won't go unnoticed by him."

The bishop had been very appreciative. The whole family had. "I did what any of us would do."

"For you, I think it was different. Watch your heart, son. Dorcas Bontrager might have returned, but she's not one of us."

He knew that, but it didn't stop the feelings growing inside him.

She'd looked so...so...Amish in that cape dress. Except for her colorful hair hanging down, she appeared every bit as Amish as anyone else.

She could be Amish again. If she wanted to be.

But she didn't want to be.

What could he say or do to convince her to stay and become Amish? "Maybe if I talked to her, I could persuade her to stay."

Vater put his hand on Eli's shoulder. "She lived in the *Englisher* world for a long time. It's hard for a person to come back from that. Don't get your hopes up, *sohn*."

Vater was right, but it was too late. Eli's hopes had already soared.

"Even if she did return to our Amish ways, how could you trust that she would stay? If she left once, she will likely leave again."

"But she would know that the outside world hadn't worked for her. She went out there to test it, and it had failed her. I— We won't fail her."

"Some people can't see that this life is the best life they can have. They always think that there is something better someplace else."

Dr. Kathleen had been out in the world far longer than Rainbow Girl had been, and she'd returned.

"I will pray for *Gott* to change her heart." And if He didn't change her heart, then He needed to change Eli's.

Chapter Thirteen

Dori had enjoyed working with Dr. Kathleen and her sister, Jessica, creating a website and database for them. Then she'd created a website for the doctor's husband, Noah, and his woodworking business. Then, as she'd gone through the websites of the different community members for her *grossvater* to review, she contacted the ones she felt she could help improve their sites.

People paid her, and she'd saved up quite a nice little nest egg. Enough to move into a small apartment in town. But then, she wouldn't have this website work with the Amish, and her baby was due in just under two months. It would be best if she stayed put until after the baby came.

Dori had outgrown even her wide-legged, split-skirt pants. She dug out the cape dresses from behind the living room end table. She didn't really have anything else to wear at this point. Maybe she should go into town to see what she could find at a thrift store. Did she really want to spend her money on clothes she would wear for only a couple of months? Clothes that would stand out among the Amish? Clothes she didn't really want?

Ne. It would take away from being able to rent an apartment.

She put on the rosy pink cape dress. She wasn't sure how to make it hang right over her growing belly, even though the gathered skirt had plenty of fabric. She fastened it the best she could and hiked across the yard to the big *haus* and knocked. Strange to knock on the door of the home she grew up in.

Mutter came around the side of the *haus*. "*Guten morgen*, Dorcas."

"*Mutter*, can you help me get this to fit right?"

Mutter's smile stretched wide. "*Ja.* Come inside." She made quick work of moving buttons and adjusting things, and soon the dress fitted *wunderbar*. "Bring me the other dress, and I can alter it, as well."

"You don't have to do that."

"I want to." *Mutter* glanced at Dori's belly.

Dori held out her hand. "Would you like to feel your grandchild move?"

"*Ja.*"

Dori placed her *mutter*'s hand on her stomach where she'd last felt the baby move. As though the child inside knew its *grossmutter* was there, it gave a high five.

Mutter sucked in a breath. "It's a strong one."

"*Ja.* Sometimes so strong it wakes me up at night or knocks the wind out of *meine* lungs." Dori was glad to be able to share this with her *mutter*. This experience would have been so different if she was still with Craig. And not for the better. She rarely thought of him anymore.

In the early evening of the Fourth of July, Dori sat on the porch of the big *haus* with Ruth. Crickets chirped in the distance. Though she wore her pink cape dress, she hadn't put her hair up nor put on a *kapp*. She studied her sister from the side.

Ruth, the perfect picture of what an Amish woman should be and look like, twisted one hand in the other, shifted her feet about and leaned forward on the bench, then back.

Dori suspected if she said boo, her sister would shoot straight up into the air, but she dared not try it. Ruth didn't need to be any more agitated. Had Dori been like this when she was younger? She'd felt giddy around Craig, but that was a long time ago. Now her giddiness came from a different source. "You're going to wear yourself out. You're wearing me out just watching you."

"I'm sorry. I'm just excited about tonight."

Though a struggle, Dori managed to keep her emotions under control.

An open buggy came up the road.

Her sister stood up. "That must be them." She peered into the *haus* through the screen door. "They're here, *Vater*." She sat back down.

The buggy pulled into the yard with Eli at the reins. Dori replayed their shared kiss the week before. Warm soft lips on hers, and strong arms around her. She'd felt safe with him. Dori's pulse quickened. The closer he came, the more her own delight wound up. If she wasn't careful, she might start twisting her hands together and shuffling her feet. Would they kiss again tonight? With fireworks shooting off overhead? She hoped so.

When the buggy stopped, both men got out.

Vater stepped forward. "You girls stay here." He went down off the porch. "I expect you boys to have *meine* daughters home at a reasonable time."

Dori lowered her head. How embarrassing.

Though Daniel looked apprehensive, Eli didn't flinch. "We're meeting up with several others, so we'll be part of a larger group. Fireworks don't start until dark. We'll return as soon as they're over."

Vater nodded. "*Gut*. I am trusting *meine* daughters with you two."

Dori wanted to spare them all some humiliation and grabbed her sister's arm. "Come on." She escorted Ruth off the porch. "We'll be fine, *Vater*."

Vater narrowed his eyes at her. "You behave."

"I will." What more trouble could she get into? She was already pregnant.

Daniel helped Ruth into the back seat and sat beside her.

Dori thrilled in anticipation of sitting next to Eli.

He took Dori's hand and assisted her into the front. "Be careful. Watch your step. Don't slip."

"I'm fine." Her accident last week rattled him more than it had her. Though her hip and ankle were both still sore, she and her baby were fine. She settled on the seat near the middle so he'd have to sit close to her.

But he managed to sit on the far edge of the seat so as not to have his arm brush against hers. Leaning forward with his elbows resting on his legs, he snapped the reins and clicked his tongue. The horse obeyed.

She wanted to calm his fears. "I really am fine. I went to the doctor's yesterday, and she said we are both doing well." She put her hand on her belly.

"I know."

Then what had him in a mood? Wait a minute. He knew? How? "What do you mean you know?"

"I stopped by the clinic and asked her if it was safe for you to be out tonight."

She wasn't sure whether to be offended by his intrusion or delighted he cared enough to ask. "So if she'd said I shouldn't go, you would have canceled?"

He swung his head sideways, and looked at her for the first time. "You wouldn't want to risk the baby, would you?"

"*Ne*, but..."

"Would you have still come if she'd said it would put the baby at risk?"

She didn't want to answer but did. *"Ne."* But she would have considered it to be near Eli.

"That wasn't a very convincing answer. Are fireworks more important than your baby's well-being?"

This conversation had gotten off track fast. "Of course, *meine* baby's more important." She wouldn't intentionally do anything that could harm her baby, but that didn't mean the thought of being near him didn't cross her mind. "I only wanted to assure you we were fine."

"If I thought I had any chance at talking you out of going tonight, I would have tried." He faced forward again.

That stung. "Why? Because you don't think I should go?"

"You should be resting for your sake and the baby's."

She wished she hadn't brought it up. Time to steer this conversation in a different direction. "I added those new items you made to your website. You have two more orders. I'll come over in the morning with the invoices, and we can box them up and take them into town to ship out."

"*Ne*. I'll come to the bishop's in the afternoon. You sleep in."

She did like the idea of sleeping in but didn't like being told what to do. She needed to let her emotions cool off before she spoiled the evening altogether. "Sleeping in will be nice." Not that she actually could with an active baby kicking her insides.

Eli did not want to be here beside Rainbow Girl. *Ne*, it wasn't that he didn't want to be beside her, it was that he wanted to keep her safe. He could do that better back at the *dawdy haus* or his forge. The images of her in the ditch still haunted him. He couldn't shake them, and he still bore the wounds in his palms where the slipping branch dug in and cut his flesh. Not bad, but still tender. How could she be so cavalier with her safety?

She looked so Amish in the cape dress, even with her colorful hair down, and he wanted to wrap her in his arms and protect her from everything. He wanted to keep her safe and close. He wanted to kiss her again.

Eli pulled the buggy to a stop in the meadow near a couple of other early arrivers. He helped Rainbow Girl out of the buggy, but he made sure not to remind her to be careful. He would just see to it she didn't slip.

With the basket of food packed by his *mutter* and a quilt to put on the grass, he led the way to a spot in the shade of an oak tree. He set the basket down and refused help from either of the girls and had Daniel help him spread the quilt on the ground.

Before even sitting on the blanket, Ruth spoke to her sister. "You want to go for a walk around the pond while we wait?"

"That would be nice."

Both girls turned to Eli and Daniel, but it was Rainbow Girl who spoke. "What about you two?"

Daniel smiled. "Sounds *gut*."

It would be better if Eli didn't go. The more he was around Rainbow Girl, the more he wanted to kiss her. This was definitely not the place for that. "I'll stay here and keep an eye on our things." Not that anyone would bother their stuff. He lowered himself to the quilt to deter anyone from trying to coax him otherwise.

Rainbow Girl's expression changed. "I'm a little tired. I think I'll stay here, as well. You two have fun."

Daniel and Ruth left without a fuss.

Rainbow Girl stepped to the edge of the quilt. "It'll be *gut* to rest."

Eli jumped to his feet and offered her a hand to help her sit safely. He couldn't tell if she was allowing the other couple to have a little time to themselves, or if she wanted to be alone with him. Well, not exactly alone in a meadow full of other Amish. "I think resting is wise." He sat again on the far side of the quilt.

"I think I've figured it out. Figured *you* out."

He quirked an eyebrow, not knowing what she was talking about. "What's that?"

"Last week, when you pulled me out of that ditch."

He pushed aside the image of her down there all muddy. "It's over with. No sense dwelling on it." He certainly didn't want to.

"But I think you're bothered by it."

"Of course I'm bothered. Who wouldn't be? You could have been seriously injured or worse. It had to be very scary for you."

"Not as much as I would have thought. It was strange. I never felt as though *meine* life was ever in any real jeopardy. *Ja*, I wondered how long I'd be stuck and how high the water trickling over *meine* feet would get, but not any real danger."

"Because *Gott* was with you."

A short laugh burst from her. "*Gott?* I doubt He bothers with me."

Eli smiled. That meant she still believed in Him. That was *gut*. "He does *bother* with you. With all of us."

She shook her head. "I didn't start this conversation to talk about Him. I wanted to talk about something else. About our kiss."

"Shh." He glanced around at the nearest Amish. "Someone might hear you."

"So? It's not a crime to kiss."

"Our people wouldn't approve. And what if your *vater* found out? He wouldn't be happy. You heard what he said when we left this evening."

"It was just a kiss."

"*Ne.* It was a *kiss.* Not something to take lightly."

She tilted her head. "A kiss doesn't have to mean anything."

Doesn't have to mean anything? It had meant a great deal to him. Had it meant nothing to her? "I think a kiss always means something."

With narrowed eyes, she studied him for a moment. "Always?"

"Always. How can something so intimate not be?"

She continued to stare at him for a while. "So if a kiss *always* means something, what did it mean to you?"

Ne, this wasn't *gut*. He didn't want to talk about

this. "I don't know. I wasn't thinking. Now, stop talking about it before someone hears you."

She shifted to face him. "Someone once told me that a kiss *always* means something, so I'll tell you what it meant to me."

Was she throwing his words back at him? "I don't want to know." But that wasn't true. He did.

"It meant that we weren't strangers. That even though I'm not technically Amish, I'm not completely cast aside."

She'd ignored his request, but it pleased him to know their kiss hadn't meant nothing to her as she had implied.

She chattered on. "I've told you. Now it's your turn."

He shook his head. He wasn't about to say any more than he already had.

She lowered her voice. "Would you like me to tell this growing crowd what we've done?"

He straightened. "You wouldn't. Your *vater* and your *grossvater* would never let you leave the *haus* again." Nor allow him to see her.

"Wouldn't I?"

He had no doubt that she would. "As I said, I wasn't thinking. I was so grateful that you were all right, but that's no excuse. I still shouldn't have done that." But he was glad he had.

All this talk made him want to kiss her again. He should have gone on that walk around the pond.

When the last fireworks faded overhead, Dori wished for more so this night would never end. The fireworks had seemed more brilliant and spectacular this year, but she didn't know why. There hadn't been anything new from years past. She just kept thinking how nice it was to share them with Eli.

People all around the meadow rose, folded up their quilts and blankets and headed for their buggies, like birds being scattered by a predator. Even Daniel and Ruth got to their feet. Eli did not.

Daniel shifted from foot to foot. "Shouldn't we get the buggy? I don't want to make Andrew or the bishop angry by not getting the girls home promptly."

Eli waved a hand toward the cluster of buggies. "Everyone's crowding around. There's not enough room for everyone to leave at the same time. Once some are on their way, there will be more room to maneuver. Do you really want to be bunched up on the road behind several other buggies?"

Dori had to hand it to Eli, he was thinking ahead. She certainly didn't mind spending a little extra time with the blacksmith.

Daniel stared at all the people swarming around the buggies. "I suppose you're right." After a couple of minutes, he spoke again. "I'm going over to check on the horse, to be ready when things clear out."

He headed off.

Ruth caught up to him. "I'll go with you, Daniel."

Dori chuckled. "Does *meine vater* scare him that much?"

"That and the man behind your *vater*." Eli stood and held out a hand to her.

She placed hers in his larger one, strong and warm. "What man?"

He pulled her to her feet with little effort on her part. "The bishop."

My, Eli *was* strong. "He's not scary." Less so since she'd returned a little over a month ago.

Holding her hand longer than necessary, he gazed down at her a moment before answering. "He's the bishop, therefore he's scary to a lot of people."

"You're not afraid of him, are you?" Would Eli try to kiss her again? No one was around or looking. They were all busy trying to leave.

"I try not to put myself in situations that would cause him to look crossly in *meine* direction."

Situations like this?

He continued without a clue as to her thoughts. "Follow the rules, and there's no need to worry."

She liked Eli's self-confidence. Part of the reason she'd left the community was the bishop's anger toward her. The more he stated his disappointment in her, the more rules she broke, the more displeased he was. On and on it went until she couldn't take it any longer, and finally left. But he had changed in her absence.

"We should head over to the buggy now." Eli released her hand and picked up the quilt.

Her hand felt empty and cold without him holding it. When she took a step, a pain shot through her injured hip, and she gasped.

Eli dropped the blanket and took her elbow. "What's wrong? Is the baby coming already?"

"*Ne. Meine* bruised hip is sore and stiff from sitting on the ground. I'm fine."

"Are you sure?"

"*Ja.* I'm sure. Go on ahead. I'll take it slow until it loosens up."

"I'll walk with you."

He didn't have to do so, but she was glad he did.

By the time they reached the buggy, half of the crowd had already cleared out, making it easier to get around the vehicle. Some of the buggies formed a line leading to the road, while others trotted their horse down the road in one direction or the other. Daniel had theirs all ready. "Do you want me to drive this time?"

Eli shook his head. "I'll drive."

Once everyone had climbed aboard and was seated in the same place as before, Eli set the horse into motion. Even with waiting, they weren't the last buggy to leave the meadow.

Dori leaned back to relieve the pressure on her lungs from the baby and to make it easier to breathe.

Eli glanced at her sideways. "Are you all right? Is your hip all right? Do you need me to stop?"

"I'm fine."

The baby within shifted to the side of her belly where Eli sat as though it was trying to get closer to him. Dori couldn't blame the little one. If Dori could figure out how, she would scoot closer, as well.

The buggy wheel dipped into a pothole, rocking the vehicle almost violently. Dori grabbed the side of the seat, then found herself pressed against Eli's side.

His arm wrapped securely around her shoulders. "Are you all right?"

"I'm fine." Better now with him closer.

"Sorry about that. I didn't see the hole in the dark."

"It couldn't be helped." Afraid he might remove his arm and pull away, she leaned her head against his shoulder.

He released the pressure around her as though he

might pull his arm away, but he couldn't without drawing attention to where he'd placed his arm. It relaxed back into place.

The swaying of the buggy lulled Dori and caused her eyelids to grow heavy.

What seemed like a moment later, his hand and arm jiggled her awake. "We're almost there."

Dori looked ahead and could see her family home.

Eli removed his arm from around her and turned in the seat to the couple in the back. "We're here."

Daniel and Ruth straightened and shifted apart.

As Eli faced front again, he scooted a couple of inches away from Dori.

Instinctively, Dori did so too. She smiled to herself. Had her parents as well Eli's and Daniel's parents done the very same thing when they were courting? Not that Eli was courting Dori, because he wasn't, but the situation would have been similar.

Vater and *Mutter* sat on the porch of the big *haus* with *Grossvater*. Sentries waiting for the wanderers to return.

A reminder of what she didn't like about the Amish, and the reasons why she wasn't staying. She needed to stop thinking of Eli the way she had been this past week and to stop dreaming about another kiss from him. No *gut* could come of it.

Dori shook her head. "They all came out to see that we behaved."

Eli chuckled beside her as he turned into the driveway and stopped in front of the big *haus*.

Daniel helped Ruth down from the buggy.

Eli gripped Dori's hand firmly. Was it because he

wanted to hold her hand? Or because he feared she might fall?

As she climbed down, her foot caught on the step, and she stumbled forward into his arms.

His embrace held her securely on her feet.

Gazing up at him, she longed for him to kiss her good-night. If there wasn't an audience, would he? *Ne.* If he did, it would have to *mean* something, and for him, it couldn't. Not as long as she wasn't Amish.

She would never become Amish.

Chapter Fourteen

The summer sped past, and now, on the last day of August, Eli sat in a chair next to Rainbow Girl at the computer in the bishop's *haus*. She was updating his website. Again. She seemed to do it every time they met. He received orders for his products regularly, thanks to her, and he was making *gut* money.

Eli tapped a price on the screen. "You are still charging people too much."

"Ne. These are market-value prices. You could probably charge even more, and *Englishers* would pay it."

"Ne." He shook his head. "You have the prices too high as it is. It doesn't cost me that much to make them."

"That's what they're worth. You have a unique skill. You make intricate, beautiful pieces and don't understand their value to the outside world. Your time and expertise are very valuable."

He harrumphed. Though he liked earning the prices she put on his work, he didn't want to cheat people.

"When are you going to get your own computer?"

She tapped on the keys. "The church leaders have approved one for you."

He didn't want his own computer. He liked working with her. "Why should I get a computer? You would be the one to have to run it for me anyway."

"You could learn."

"I don't want to learn. I only want to make things out of hot iron." If it weren't for spending time with her, he wouldn't be doing any of this.

She drew in a quick, soft breath as she had done every few minutes for the past hour and a half.

"Are you all right?"

Nodding, she released the air in her lungs. "I'm fine. These are what people tell me are practice contractions. Braxton Hicks."

His breath caught in his throat, and his insides galloped like a runaway horse. "Is the baby coming? Now?"

"Ne, ne." She pushed her chair away from the table and stood. "I'll be right back." When she reached the hallway, she gripped the wall and bent over, sucking in air between her teeth.

Eli jumped up and hurried to her side. "You aren't all right, are you?"

She didn't answer but shook her head, then contradicted that action with a nod.

Was that a *ja* or *ne*? "I don't know what that means. Tell me what to do."

A moment later, she straightened and breathed normally. "I think that might have been more than practice. It was a lot stronger than the others."

"What do you mean?"

"I think I'm in labor."

"The baby's coming?" Eli jerked his head about, looking around. "Where's the bishop?"

"Out visiting, but he wouldn't be much *gut*. Go to the big *haus* and tell *meine mutter*."

"All right." He dashed for the door.

"Eli?" Rainbow Girl's strained voice stopped him in his tracks.

He swung around. "What?"

"Would you bring me a chair?"

He brought her one of the straight-backed ones from the table. "Maybe I shouldn't leave you."

"Unless you plan to deliver this baby, get *Mutter*. Now."

He swallowed hard and ran out the door. He pounded on the door of the big *haus*. When no answer came, he let himself in. *"Hallo?"* Nobody replied, and a quick search yielded an empty *haus*.

He ran back to the *dawdy haus*.

Rainbow Girl still sat in the chair at the entrance to the hall.

"Your *mutter* wasn't there. No one was." That meant there were two lives in his hands, Rainbow Girl's and her baby's. "I don't know how to help you. What should I do? I can go get someone else."

She shook her head. "That would take too long. Go hitch up a buggy and drive me to the clinic."

He breathed easier. He wasn't going to have to... *Don't think about it.*

He'd never hitched up a buggy so fast. He pulled it to the front of the *dawdy haus* and ran inside.

Rainbow Girl stood with her hands braced on the table, breathing erratically and moaning.

"Please don't have the baby right now."

Rainbow Girl shook her head, and her breathing steadied. "I'm fine. Just get me to the doctor's." She took a step and faltered.

This would be too slow. Eli scooped her up into his arms. "How many pains have you had while I was getting the buggy?"

"Just that one."

Gut. There was still time.

He carried Rainbow Girl to the waiting buggy. After placing her on the seat, he climbed in and set the horse into motion. When the vehicle jerked forward, she sucked in a breath.

"What is it? What's wrong?"

She spoke through gritted teeth. "Too bumpy."

"I can't help that. Do you want me to stop?"

"*Ne.* Just keep going. Get me there as fast as you can."

He urged Dutch to pull the buggy as quickly as he could.

A few minutes down the road, Rainbow Girl straightened. "Go back. I left *meine* phone on the table."

"*Ne.*"

"But we should call ahead to the clinic and let them know we're coming."

She was thinking like the *English*.

"*Ne.*" He couldn't risk her having the baby in the buggy. That would be bad. "The doctor will understand us coming unannounced."

Rainbow Girl gripped his arm. "Eli?"

"*Ja.*"

"I'm scared."

He was too, more than he could have imagined.

"Everything will be all right." As long as they arrived in time.

"Danki."

He prayed the whole way while keeping one eye on Rainbow Girl. It seemed like forever before the clinic came into view. *Please, let the doctor be there.* A buggy sat out front. *Gut.* That likely meant that she had a patient and was there. He hauled back on the reins until the horse stopped. He set the brake and scooped Rainbow Girl up into his arms again.

"I can walk." She sucked in a breath between her teeth.

"This is faster." The sooner he could turn her over to someone else's care—someone who knew what to do—the better for both of them, *ne*, all three of them. But he rather liked having her in his arms.

Rainbow Girl turned the knob, and he pushed the door open with his foot.

The Miller family crowded the waiting area.

Moaning came from one of the rear rooms.

A loud female voice called from the same vicinity, "I can't see any other patients right now. You'll have to come back tomorrow."

Eli glanced from one wide-eyed Miller face to another. He spoke to them. "We can't. She's having a baby."

Deborah Miller wove between her family members and trotted to the back.

Young, almond-eyed Sarah Miller, the youngest, stood next to Eli and stared up at him. *"Mutter* is having our baby now."

"Oh, dear." What would that mean for Rainbow Girl?

Rainbow Girl patted his hand. "Set me down."

Before he could, Dr. Kathleen came out. "Busy day. Bring her into *meine* office."

Eli followed the doctor.

"Have her sit in a chair until *meine* husband can pull down the extra bed."

Eli gingerly lowered Rainbow Girl to her feet. "I can do that."

"That would be *gut*. I'll send *meine* sister in to help you." The doctor smiled at the *mutter*-to-be. "How far apart are your contractions?"

"A few minutes or so."

"They come about every seven or eight minutes." He'd been timing them on the ride here. "They're getting closer all the time."

Both women stared at him for a moment.

"What?" When his youngest sister was on the way, it had been Eli's job to time the contractions while his *vater* went for the midwife.

The doctor nodded. "I'll return in a few minutes. I'll send Jessica in. Keep timing her contractions." She left.

A moment later, Jessica entered and walked to Rainbow Girl. "We need to move you to the end of the desk beside the bookcase to make room for the bed. Let me know when the next contraction ends?"

Rainbow Girl nodded.

"She's about to start one." It had been nearly seven minutes since the last one.

Rainbow Girl pinned him with a stare. "How do you know?"

"I have a *gut* sense of time." He held up his wrist. "And a watch."

Rainbow Girl sucked in a breath. "He's right." She moaned.

Eli couldn't wait, grabbing the back of her chair and pulling it along with her into place. "Why does she need to be over here?"

Jessica moved across the room and pointed toward the top of the paneled wall. "There are wooden catches on each side that need to be turned vertical. Then the Murphy bed can be lowered."

He twisted the catches and lowered the bed.

Jessica held up an index finger. "Oops! Let me go grab some bed linens and a pillow." She did and had the bed made in a snap.

After Rainbow Girl's next contraction, Eli carried her, against her protests, to the bed and set her on it.

"You know I can still walk."

"Not when one of those pains hits you. It's faster if I carry you, then you don't risk falling." He pointed toward the door. "I'll wait out there."

Jessica stood in his way. "Stay with her until Dr. Kathleen comes in. It's best if she's not alone." She skittered out of the room.

He stared after her. He didn't want to stay. He didn't know what to do. With the Murphy bed down, there wasn't much space to move around, so he sat on the edge of the desk and watched for signs of the onset of another pain.

"Stop staring at me."

He couldn't. "I don't know what else to do."

"Talk to me."

"What do you want me to say?"

"I don't care. Talk about your family. Tell me a story. Why you like being a blacksmith. Anything."

"We needed a blacksmith in our community. Ours

had passed away, and I don't care so much for farming. Don't tell anyone."

She smiled at that, and he continued to tell her about how he got started, learning from a neighboring community's blacksmith.

Dr. Kathleen came in, and he stood.

She pointed toward the door. "You can wait in the other room."

Finally. He escaped as quickly as possible before the doctor changed her mind.

The Miller family occupied all the seats. Eli would rather stand anyway.

Deborah Miller also stood. "*Meine vater* and Amos are in the barn with Noah Lambright. You could go join them if you like."

He would love to retreat with the other men. "I'll do that after the doctor tells me how she's doing."

It seemed like forever before Dr. Kathleen emerged. He checked his watch. Had it been only a few minutes? He crossed to her. "How is she?"

"She's doing fine. It will be a little while yet. Why don't you go sit with her?"

"Me?"

She patted his arm. "She'll be less scared if she's not alone."

But *he* wouldn't. "Why not one of these women?"

"Because she asked for you." The doctor walked into the first room with her other *mutter* in labor.

Eli took a deep breath and entered the one with Rainbow Girl in it. He smiled. "How are you?"

"Apparently, I haven't had nearly enough of these pains that feel as though I'm being ripped in half. It might be a while yet before the baby comes. *And* the pains will probably get a lot worse. How is that possible? I already feel like I'm going to die with each one."

He did *not* want to see her in any more pain. He cocked his thumb toward the door. "There are several women out there. I'm sure any of them would be happy to come in here with you. You'd probably be more comfortable with one of them."

"If you don't mind, I'd like you to stay with me."

He did mind. "Of course, I'll stay. Whatever you want." He sat on the edge of the desk again.

"I don't really know those women. I mean I know them, but I don't really *know* them." She sucked in a breath between her teeth.

He fell to his knees beside the bed and took her hand. "Squeeze it as hard as you like. I can take it."

She did.

And it actually hurt.

Two hours later, Teresa Miller in the next room had a baby boy named Micah. After seven girls, Bartholomew Miller finally had a son. He must be more than pleased.

Four hours after that, Eli continued to pace in the waiting area. As it had turned out, the rush to get to the clinic hadn't needed to be so rushed after all. Rainbow Girl had been offered the chance to go to the hospital in Goshen, but she turned it down as long as she had Dr. Kathleen. Rainbow Girl screamed in pain every minute or two, but fortunately her parents were there. Her *mutter* at her side and her *vater* pacing with Eli in the waiting area. They glanced at one another every third pass or so. The bishop sat in an overstuffed armchair, head back, eyes closed. How could he be so relaxed?

It seemed like forever had passed before a cry finally heralded the birth of the second baby that day.

Eli's breath released in a rush of relief.

When Rainbow Girl's *vater* was invited to go in and see his daughter and grandchild, Eli slumped onto the love seat, completely worn-out. How could he be this exhausted? He hadn't done anything. Rainbow Girl had to be utterly spent. How had she done this all day?

He didn't know how long he'd sat there before the doctor came out. He stood. "How is she?"

The bishop stood, as well.

She nodded. "*Mutter* and daughter are doing fine."

"And what about the baby? Is it a boy or girl?"

She smiled with a hint of a laugh behind it. "A girl."

Eli smiled back. "A little girl."

"Would you like to go in and see them?"

Ja, he would but was tentative. "I don't want to bother anyone."

"Let me ask." She disappeared and returned quickly. "She wants you to come in."

The bishop patted his arm. "Tell Andrew and Leah that I'm heading home and will let the other children know." He left.

Eli followed the doctor into the room and told them the bishop had gone home.

Her *mutter* sat in a chair beside the bed, and her *vater* stood behind her *mutter*, gazing down at his daughter and *enkelin*. He seemed pleased.

Though Rainbow Girl wore a huge smile, the dark circles under her slowly drooping eyes spoke of her exhaustion. "Meet *meine* daughter, Tabitha."

"That's a beautiful name for a beautiful baby girl."

"Would you like to hold her?"

"Me? *Ne*. I don't think that's a *gut* idea."

Leah Bontrager stood and motioned him over. "Sit. It will be all right."

Eli looked to Andrew Bontrager. When the older man gave him a nod, Eli sat. Rainbow Girl handed over the sleeping bundle. He gazed upon her tiny, scrunched-up face and instantly fell in love with the little one. He would do anything to protect her.

And her *mutter*.

Rainbow Girl.

Now she had to stay and join church. She just had to. What would he do if she left?

Dori regarded Eli holding Tabitha in the chair next to the bed. The big, strapping, muscle-bound black-smith holding a tiny, helpless newborn. She trusted him completely with her daughter. She suddenly realized that she should tell Craig that he had a daughter. But would he even care? The man sitting here next to her cared more for her daughter than the little one's own *vater*. "*Danki* for looking after me and Tabitha."

"I didn't do anything. The doctor did everything."

"You kept us safe and got us here." She had never felt more secure than with him.

He gave a crooked smile. "Turns out, there wasn't such a rush to get you here after all. Sorry about all the bumps in the road."

"Couldn't be helped. Getting us here gave us both peace of mind."

He returned his gaze to the bundle in his arms. "She's perfect." He spoke like a proud *vater*.

But Dori knew that could never be.

Dr. Kathleen came to the doorway. "With two new *mutters* and babies to look after, we've made up beds in the big *haus*. I would like to get both of you over there as soon as possible. Ladies have come and fixed a *wunderbar* supper. It will be easier to care for you there overnight."

Dori turned from Eli and her daughter to the doctor. "I don't want to inconvenience you. I can go home."

The doctor shook her head. "That's not a *gut* idea. You seem fine, but I should keep an eye on your baby at least overnight. Things can develop quickly with these little ones. The beds in the big *haus* are more comfortable, and I'll be closer." She held up her hand. "I'll hear no further arguments. The Millers are helping Teresa and Micah over there right now."

Staying at Dr. Kathleen's *haus* eased Dori's concerns. She wasn't sure how to care for her new baby yet, though *Mutter* would help.

The doctor pointed to Eli. "Hand the baby to Leah. I need you to help Dori across the yard. She needs someone to support her."

Dori liked the idea of holding on to Eli for support. He *was* strong.

He turned Tabitha over to her *grossmutter*, scooped Dori up into his arms and stood. "Lead the way."

The doctor laughed.

Dori hooked her arms around his neck. She didn't mind being in his arms.

The whole parade of them marched toward the big *haus*.

Once upstairs, Eli deposited her on a big, comfortable bed. Much better than the thin mattress of the Murphy bed.

After a tasty supper of chicken and dumplings, everyone left, except a couple of members of the Miller family, Dori's *mutter* and Eli. He decided to stay for a little longer.

She fed Tabitha and stopped resisting her heavy eyelids. It had been a long day.

Dori woke to a baby crying in the distance and the dawning light drifting in through the open curtains. Where was Tabitha? Dori glanced around. Where was she? This was not the *dawdy haus*, but the doctor's home.

Dori's *mutter* lay curled on the bed next to her. But where was her baby?

She turned her head to the other side.

Eli sat on the floor with his head leaning against the wall, asleep. Cradled in his crossed legs, Tabitha lay snuggled up and sleeping too. One gigantic hand on the top of her little head, and the other hooked around her blanketed legs. She breathed a sigh of relief. The crying baby was not hers.

Mutter rose up on one elbow and moved a stray strand of hair from Dori's face. She indicated the sleeping giant and whispered, "He was up walking her during the night. He'll make a *gut vater*."

Was her *mutter* hinting? Eli would make a *gut vater*, but he could never be Tabitha's. He deserved someone better than Dori. A *gut* Amish wife. A wife who would give him his own children and not those of another man. Worse, an *English* man.

For now, she would be content to watch the two sleep. Soon enough this tranquil atmosphere would be shattered. First by a baby crying, then by Dori's leaving.

Chapter Fifteen

Two weeks after Tabitha's birth, Dori traveled into town with Eli, who had orders he needed to ship. Since her daughter's arrival, he spent a lot of time at *Grossvater*'s *haus* and stopped by every day, even if only for a few minutes. He spent a lot of time with Tabitha. And even more time with Dori. There was always some excuse or other for coming to the *haus*. She didn't care what the reason. She enjoyed his company.

Dori's hair had grown out and looked terrible. She planned to buy hair dye today and make it all one color. She hadn't decided which one yet. Maybe she would choose pink for the whole thing in honor of having a daughter.

Eli stopped in the drugstore parking lot. "Would you like me to go in with you?"

Dori gazed down at her daughter in her arms. "She's asleep. I hate to disturb her."

"I'll take her." He set the brake, got out and came around to her side of the vehicle.

"You really want to?"

"Ja." He held out his arms. It was such a change

from two weeks ago, on the day of her birth. He'd been terrified to hold her, but he had quickly gotten over that.

She placed her daughter in the safety of his strong arms. "I won't be long." Now he looked comfortable and at ease holding a baby. It warmed Dori's heart. *"Danki."*

Though she didn't want to part from either of them, she dashed inside the drugstore and surveyed the options. No pink, purple, blue, orange or green. This wasn't the kind of store to carry such colors.

She wouldn't be Rainbow Girl much longer. That saddened her. Eli had given her that affectionate name. She didn't want to lose her fun hair colors. She wanted to be Rainbow Girl. Eli's Rainbow Girl. But she couldn't. As long as she remained Rainbow Girl, she could never hope to be Eli's.

She studied the options and picked up a box that was close to her natural color. That would be something different. If she couldn't have an unusual color, she might as well go back to her natural one.

Grossvater had been so kind to her, and her *vater* even started speaking to her again. It would be nice to give something back to all of them, her *grossvater*, her parents, her family, the whole community. To Eli. She could always color it different colors again later— after she left—but for now, she needed to stay with the Amish. She couldn't bear to be parted from her little girl.

She purchased the hair color and headed outside to meet up with Eli. He seemed to love little Tabitha, and loved holding her as much as Dori did. He would make someone a *gut* husband and *vater* someday. At the thought of him married to someone else, a pang twisted inside her. Hopefully, she wouldn't be around to witness that.

She headed across the parking lot toward the buggy.

"Dori?"

She recognized that voice and spun around. "Craig?" She couldn't believe, after all these months, she was finally seeing him again.

"I see you've had the baby. Or did you…?"

Have an abortion? "I told you, I would never do that. I had the baby. Two weeks ago."

He took her hands in his. "Great. Then you're coming home?"

"You want us back?" She'd dreamed of this, but she hadn't truly expected it. He'd changed his mind after all.

"Just you. Leave the kid with the Amish people."

Leave her child? How could he ask that? "If you could just—"

"Don't say it. I don't want to see it. I don't want to know." He squeezed her hands. "It hasn't been right without you. I've missed you so much. I haven't eaten well. I don't sleep. I feel lost without you."

Part of her wanted to fall into his arms and leave *everything* else behind. When she thought of only him, she imagined she could. "If you missed me so much, why didn't you come for me?"

He shrugged one shoulder. "I didn't know how to find you."

Didn't know how? "You could have asked *any* Amish person where the Bontragers lived, and they could have told you."

He scrunched up his face. "I don't want to talk to *those* people."

She couldn't believe him and pulled her hands free. "*I'm* one of *those* people."

He held out his hands. "But you're different."

"Not that different." Not as different as she'd thought.

"Wearing their clothes doesn't make you Amish. Even with your hair pulled back and under that funny hat, I can tell you still have it all different colors. That's how I could tell it was you. It lets me know you aren't one of them."

She had taken to wearing the more comfortable cape dresses since her experience in the ditch, and since Tabitha's birth, putting her hair up in a *kapp* was easier. The weight of the hair color in her bag grounded her in this moment. She wouldn't have rainbow hair much longer.

"Stop hiding with those people and come home. Dori, I love you. I don't want to live without you."

He was right. She had been hiding with the Amish, but no more. "But you don't want our child?"

"How can I? I don't even know it."

It? Anger boiled inside her. "Our child is not an *it*. Do you even want to know if you have a son or a daughter?"

He held his hands out to his sides. "I can't afford to. *I* don't have a child. I don't make enough to support three people right now. Later, when we can buy a house, then we can have a kid."

"What about the one we already have? Do we somehow forget that one?" She couldn't.

"Obviously, *you* can't do that. We can leave it with

your Amish relatives, and when we get a house, we'll go and get it."

It? He acted like their daughter was a piece of furniture. "And how long would that be?"

"Two, maybe three years. Five tops. It will walk and talk by then, and no diapers." He gave a triumphant smile.

"You expect me to give up my child for *five* years?" Five days would be a challenge.

"You make it sound like we'd be leaving it on the side of the road. The Amish people would take care of it."

"It, it, it. Our— My child is not an it. *Auf Wiedersehen.*"

"I don't know what that means."

"*Gut* bye." She turned to leave.

"Can't we at least talk about this?"

She faced him again. "Unless there is any chance of you changing your mind, there's no point, because I'm not changing mine."

He took her hands again. "Why do you have to be so rigid? I'm sure we can come to some sort of compromise."

Compromise? That gave her hope. Was he really willing to compromise?

In the shade of a tree, Eli cradled Tabitha in his arms. The man talking to Rainbow Girl must be her old boyfriend, Tabitha's *vater*. He'd seen the joy on Rainbow Girl's face when she first saw the man, and he'd taken her hands in his. And now she wore a smile of what looked like contentment.

She'd said Tabitha's *vater* didn't want her. Did he

want her now? Eli didn't want to give the little bundle up. She'd climbed into his heart from her first breath in this world. Before that, when her *mutter* had stolen his heart.

Would Rainbow Girl leave? He didn't know how he would go on if she did. And she would take his Tabitha with her. He didn't want to lose this little one. Or her *mutter*.

Rainbow Girl strode away from the man and marched up to Eli. She stretched out her arms and spoke in English instead of *Deutsch*. "Give me my daughter."

Why? Was she going to leave with that man right now? He pulled his Rainbow Baby closer and spoke softly in *Deutsch*. "I'll hold her." He walked off toward the buggy.

She trotted to catch up. "Seriously? You're not going to give her to me."

She seemed too upset to hold one so helpless. "I don't mind holding her."

"You realize she's *meine* daughter, don't you?"

One of the many reasons he loved Tabitha so much. How could a *vater* not love her and want her?

At the buggy, he opened the door for Rainbow Girl. She climbed in and held out her arms. Instead of handing over Tabitha, he closed the door, walked around the buggy and climbed in the other side.

Rainbow Girl once again held out her arms. "I'll take her now. You can't drive while holding her."

He was sure he could, but it might not be the safest for his little one. "I'm not driving."

"What do you mean?"

He settled in the seat. "*Meine* hands are full." He looked at Rainbow Girl and nodded toward the reins.

She touched her chest with her fingertips. "You want me to drive?"

"Well, I obviously can't."

She huffed a laugh. "Are all men so stubborn?" She gathered up the reins, backed the horse up and set the buggy into motion.

He didn't know how much longer he would have his Tabitha and her *mutter* in his life. Rainbow Girl clearly still had feelings for the *Englisher*. The pain of that hit him in the center of his chest. How would he manage without them? Without her?

Once at the bishop's *haus*, Rainbow Girl fed Tabitha and put her in the crib.

Eli pointed to the computer. "Teach me how to work *meine* website."

"I thought you didn't want to learn. You didn't want to mess with *Englisher* things."

"I've changed *meine* mind. Teach me." If she was going to leave, he needed to master it like he'd done with blacksmithing. Why hadn't he learned his website from the start like she'd tried to make him do repeatedly? He'd actually acquired quite a bit of knowledge sitting next to her the past three months, but not enough to take care of it solo.

"Right now?"

"*Ja.*" He'd wanted her to think he couldn't do it himself so he could spend more time with her, and she would realize she needed to stay in their Amish community. Because, if he needed her to tend to his site, she would be around him and he would get to see her often. He would always have an excuse to come see her. He could keep her close. But he couldn't any longer. She would leave. Leave him behind. Again. "Teach me before you leave."

"What? I'm not leaving."

But she was. Why was she lying? "From the day you arrived, you insisted that you weren't staying. I need to learn how to work the website before you go."

"What brought this up all of a sudden?"

Though he didn't want to talk about him, he seemed to have little choice. "I saw you with that man."

She squinted. "What man?"

"The *Englisher* in town."

"Craig?"

"Is that his name? Is he Tabitha's *vater*?"

She took a deep breath. "*Ja.* He's her *vater*, but that doesn't mean I'm leaving."

"*Ja.* It does. I tried to deny you would leave, but I saw you with him. I saw how happy you were to see him. He was happy to see you too. He wants you back, doesn't he?"

"Well, *ja*, but…"

He'd thought it had hurt the first time she left, and he hadn't been in love with her then. Not really. Now would be a hundred times worse, because she would take Tabitha along with his heart. "But what? If he would take your daughter, would you return to him?"

She stared at him for a long moment. "He doesn't want Tabitha, so it doesn't matter."

"So if he wants you but not her, what does he expect you to do with your daughter?" When she didn't answer, he prodded. "What? Tell me."

"Leave her here with the Amish."

"You would do that?"

"*Ne.* I could never leave her behind."

"But if he wanted her?"

"He doesn't. You don't have to worry about me leaving. I'm staying for now."

"Because you have to? Why don't you leave her and go back to that man?" He waved a hand in the air. "I'll take care of Tabitha and raise her."

"You?" she chuffed out.

"Why not me?"

"Well, for one, you're a man. Two, *meine mutter* would fight you for her and likely win. Three, I'm not giving her up. Not for Craig. And not for you."

But if the *Englisher* wanted Tabitha, Rainbow Girl would return to him and be packing right now. He'd seen it on her face when she first saw him. Eli needed to get away from her and stormed off out the front door.

"What about your website?"

He didn't stop.

Each step Eli took away from Dori twisted her heart more painfully. "Eli, wait." She hurried to catch up to him and planted herself in his path. "I'm not going back to him."

He stared hard at her for a long moment. "I want to believe that."

"But?"

"I can't. I saw you with him. You still love him. Have you merely been toying with *meine* affections?"

She'd thought she still loved Craig but realized it was more of a pattern of thoughts at this point. There were no real feelings behind them anymore.

When Craig had suggested she leave Tabitha behind and return to him without her, she knew she could never go back to Craig. An invisible weight she hadn't known she carried fell away. A tether snapped. She'd broken free of him and what she'd had with him. In truth, it had been empty and meaningless. What she thought she had with him, she actually *did* have with Eli. Or at least *had*.

"I don't love him anymore. I don't know if I ever really did. I had silly notions of the outside world, and I thought Craig fulfilled those. But they were all empty." She took his hand. "Everything I want is right here."

He pulled free. "*Ne.* It's not. You want him and the *Englisher* world. I will *never* be able to trust you." He walked away.

She hurried to catch up to him. "*Ne.* Don't say that."

Tabitha's wail cut through the air.

"Go take care of your daughter." He walked away.

She wanted to follow, but her daughter needed her. She didn't want Eli to leave. She might never get him back, but if she didn't tend to her daughter, Eli wouldn't see her as a *gut mutter*. She hated having to choose between them, but there was only one choice. She turned back toward the *dawdy haus*.

After feeding, changing and getting Tabitha to sleep, Dori took the hair color she'd purchased in town to the bathroom and stood in front of the mirror. With her hair up and her *kapp* on, she looked Amish. Her roots had grown long enough that when she twisted the front, pulled everything back and secured it on the back of her head, her brown roots covered half of it. What wasn't covered, her *kapp* disguised. She removed it now and took out the bobby pins.

Her hair looked awful in all its contrasting colors and kinking in different directions. It was as though it didn't know what to do or be. Should it be up or down? So it stuck out all over. Should it be Amish or *English*? Both, with neither truly winning the battle. A confused mess. Just like her.

Eli's words echoed in her mind. *I will* never *be able to trust you.* That couldn't be true. But Eli believed it. Would she ever be able to change his mind? Not like this.

After brushing through her hair, she took the dye and a towel to the kitchen sink. This was the closest shade she could find to her natural one. Hopefully, it would cover the various colors.

When she was finished and her hair mostly dry, *Grossvater* came inside. "Your hair."

"What do you think?"

He smiled. "It looks *wunderbar.*"

The dye had covered most of the colors while others gave it a strange shade. "Once I put it up and cover it with *meine kapp*, no one should be able to tell."

"You will look like a proper Amish, then."

Did she want to? For Eli? Would *he* view her as a proper Amish woman?

The next day, the Saturday before Joining Sunday, Eli beat on the piece of hot steel on his anvil, bending it around and around and folding it over on itself. Another one ruined. He doused it in the barrel of water, then tossed it onto the pile with the other carnage from his foul mood. It clanged and clattered as it settled into place.

As he reached for another iron rod, he froze.

Rainbow Girl stood at the entrance to his blacksmith

workshop with Tabitha swaddled in her arms. What was she doing here?

"*Hallo*, Eli."

He resisted the urge to go to her and gave her a curt nod instead. "Do you have a horse who needs shoeing?"

"*Ne*. I— We came to see you."

Like iron being drawn to a magnet, he gravitated to her and Tabitha. He scooped Rainbow Baby up into his arms. This was where his little one belonged, but she would be taken away from him all too soon. He handed her over. "Why have you come?"

Rainbow Girl removed her *kapp*.

"What are you doing? You aren't supposed to do that."

She turned around. "See? I dyed *meine* hair back to its natural color."

A *gut* start, but anyone could appear Amish on the outside. "Why are you showing me?"

"So you could see that I'm becoming Amish. I can join church tomorrow."

Unless she didn't. She'd said *can*, not that she *was* going to.

"You think that changing your hair makes you Amish? It takes a lot more than that. It's not what's on the outside, it's what's in your heart. And your heart is *English*. Go back to where you belong and leave us be."

"I want to show you that you can trust me."

"*Ne*. Every time I do, you crush *meine* heart under your foot."

"When have I ever done that?"

"I've liked you since we were twelve. You went wild on *Rumspringa*, but I thought you would settle down like most Amish youths do. Instead, you left the community. I kept waiting for you to return, a few months passed, then a year, but you didn't come back. Then one day, I realized I no longer expected you to return."

"But I did."

"Only because you were forced to. And you've never really returned in your heart." He thumped his chest with his fingertips. "You keep looking over your shoulder to the *Englisher* world. Why don't you go back to Tabitha's *vater*?"

"How many times do I have to tell you that he doesn't want her, and I don't love him?"

Until she believed it herself. "You don't want the Amish life. Leave your baby with us. Go back to your *English* life. Everyone wins."

"But I don't want to leave her."

"Think of what's best for your daughter. She will have so much love here." He wanted to beg Rainbow Girl to stay, but unless she *wanted* to, she wouldn't stay for long.

Back at the *dawdy haus*, Dori paced in her bedroom while *Mutter* softly sang a hymn to Tabitha in the other room.

Eli had been right. Dori did keep looking back to the *English* world. Which one did she want to belong to? The Amish one that had taken her in and cared for her and her baby when they needed help most? Or the *English* one, where her baby's *vater* was? Craig would welcome her if she left Tabitha behind. Her baby would be well cared for and loved. She would have a *gut* life. Didn't her daughter deserve that?

If Eli hadn't been so hurt and upset about her talking

to Craig and was willing to give her a chance, she would stay. If he asked her to, she would stay. She would join church.

But if Craig would welcome and love their daughter, she would return to the *English* world. So where she ended up depended on a man? Which man would love her?

That wasn't right. A decision like this should be made by what she wanted. Did she want Craig? Or Eli? *Ne.* Did she want an *English* life with or without Craig? Or did she want an Amish life, with or without Eli?

She wanted security. Could either man give her that?

Maybe she *should* leave Tabitha behind so her daughter could have a *gut* life, a better life without Dori, and walk away from them all. Start over in a different town. Away from the Amish and away from Craig.

She fingered the door knocker. The thing that had tied her two worlds together. The thing that had kept an open door in her mind to the Amish world.

She sat on her bed and counted the money earned from helping so many Amish with their websites and computers. She hadn't done anything special, ran a few programs to get rid of viruses and malware and defragged their hard drives. But each person had paid her a fee. She had enough to rent a small apartment. Her biggest obstacle would be to find a job.

When she left, she would no longer have regular income from computer work. No Amish would be allowed to come to her for help. She would need other means to support her and her baby. Work that would pay enough for living expenses as well as child-care. How would she ever be able to afford that? She wouldn't. So she either needed to resign her fate to remaining with the Amish for the next eighteen years, or leave Tabitha here until she could provide for her. Dori disliked both options. But as Eli had said, she needed to think of what was best for her daughter above all else. She had her GED now, so she should have better success finding a job.

She left her room and stopped at the end of the hall before entering the living room.

Mutter sat in the rocking chair, singing as she gazed at Tabitha.

Dori's eyes watered at the scene. "You'll always look after her, won't you?"

"Of course. Both of you." *Mutter*'s expression changed from happy to worried. "Why do you ask this? You will take care of your daughter."

Dori wanted to but couldn't see how. "I don't think I can stay."

"Ne." Tears filled *Mutter*'s eyes. "You can't leave again. It will break your *vater*'s heart. It will break *meine* heart."

"I don't fit in here." Just when she thought she and Eli might have a chance, Craig had spoiled it, but she couldn't blame Eli after the life she'd lived outside the community.

"What about your daughter?"

That hurt most of all. "I can't take care of her out there. I'll come back for her."

"Ne. This is wrong."

Everything about her life the past few years had been wrong. Everything except Tabitha.

"You aren't leaving right now, are you?"

"Ne." She needed to make a few plans. "But soon. Don't tell anyone."

"How can I not? Your *vater* should be told, as well as your *grossvater.*"

"Ne. You can't tell them. Promise you won't tell anyone. Promise right now, or I'll take Tabitha this minute and walk out the door. You'll never see either of us again."

Mutter gasped. "I don't like this one bit."

"But you won't say anything?"

"I will keep your secret."

Dori had told Eli she could never leave her daughter behind, but here she was planning to do just that. But not forever. Only until she could make a *gut* life for her, so she could take care of her the way she needed.

Chapter Sixteen

At church the next day, with her plans set, Dori wanted the service to be over quickly. Wanted this whole day to be over so she could leave. Leave this world behind her—for *gut* this time. Except to return for Tabitha. But if she couldn't find work that could support them both, her daughter would be better off remaining here.

She shook her head. She couldn't think that way. Tabitha might be better off staying here, but Dori wouldn't be better off without her. In order to provide for her daughter, Dori needed to find a *gut*-paying job and get settled in a place, then she could return for her little girl. But even when she had all that and came back for her, how much would she really see of her daughter if she had to pay for someone else to look after her all day.

As the rest of the family headed toward the *haus*, *Vater* asked Dori to remain. "Your *mutter* said I should speak to you."

"She did? About what?" *Mutter* wasn't supposed to tell anyone about her plans to leave.

"I assume about your decision today."

So *Mutter* hadn't told him of her plans.

"Make the right one, and all will be well." *Vater* strode off.

She wished she knew what that was.

Eli stood off in the distance but ducked away when she made eye contact.

Inside, Dori sat between her sister and her *mutter*, who held Tabitha. Decision Sunday had come, and she had made hers. She would start over someplace new.

Service was at the Hochstetlers'. Eli's family's home. She wished it could have been someplace different. It had been hard seeing him. If she could have skipped church without raising suspicions, she would have. But she needed to keep up a front so she could escape unnoticed.

The bishop spoke of the importance of joining church. It had to be of one's own free will, but families put much pressure on their children to join. Joining for Dori would be wrong, because she would do it to show Eli he could trust her. That was the wrong reason. Besides, he hadn't even been able to look at her this morning.

What was the right reason? Because she wanted to be Amish? What did it mean to *be* Amish? What did it really mean to join church?

The bishop continued with his sermon. "If you feel *Gott* calling to your heart, you are ready to join church."

She'd heard this every year growing up. She'd never paid it much attention because it didn't pertain to her. And again this year, it had no bearing on her future. She would leave as soon as she could make the arrangements. Maybe as soon as Monday or Tuesday. She had her money as well as her GED. Which direction did she want to go? West. Fewer Amish.

She didn't want to leave Eli. She didn't want to leave Tabitha. She didn't want to leave *Gott*.

Gott? What did He have to do with this decision? Then she realized—everything. *Gott* was the reason to stay. *Gott* was the reason to join church. Her whole life, she'd viewed the Amish life by what others expected of her. *Gott* was the reason for everything. His was the only expectation that mattered. She finally understood what it meant to be Amish. It wasn't about what she wore or what she did or even following the *Ordnung*. It was about belonging to *Gott*, being loved and cherished by Him. For the first time in her life, she truly wanted to be Amish. To belong to *Gott*.

"Who among you will come forward to join?"

Dori's insides leaped up, but she forced her body to remain seated. She wanted to stand but didn't feel worthy. She hadn't understood what it meant to be Amish or to join church, but now she did. She wished she could go back and retake the classes to view everything her *grossvater* had said in light of her revelation that *Gott* should be the center of everything. Everything she did, thought or became. He was the reason for life.

For the first time that morning, Dori focused on *Grossvater*. He stared at her with a sad expression. He'd hoped she would join and wore his disappointment clearly on his face. She would wait until next year, when she could take the joining classes again to really understand and learn about *Gott*.

Instead, she obeyed the still-quiet voice in her heart and rose to her feet. This was why she'd twisted her hair up and put it under a *kapp*. The reason she'd removed all of her earrings. She'd obeyed that little voice inside her that had told her to do those things. It hadn't been her rebellious side as she had thought, telling her to fool everyone into thinking she'd decided to stay when she hadn't. It had been *Gott* preparing her, making her ready.

Mutter sucked in a soft breath.

Giving a nod, Dori walked to the front and knelt with the others.

Grossvater had never worn such a huge smile.

She sought out Eli. When she found him, his scowl told her all she needed to know. He didn't approve of her being up there. He didn't think she was *gut* enough. He didn't think she was Amish enough.

Gott didn't ask her to be *gut* enough or Amish enough. He wanted her to be obedient to Him. He wanted her to join church, so she would do it for Him.

She prayed Eli would come around.

When the service ended, Dori stood and turned around, anxious to talk to Eli. But he was gone.

Mutter bounced a fussy Tabitha in her arms. "I think she's hungry."

Dori took her daughter and held her close. "I'll find a room to feed her in." Eli would have to wait.

While Dori fed her little one, *Mutter* brought in a plate of food.

Once Tabitha had a full tummy and a clean diaper, Dori headed outside. She searched the crowd for Eli but couldn't spot him, so she crossed to her *vater* and oldest brother. "Have you seen Eli? I can't spot him."

"I haven't seen him." Her *vater* gave her a big smile. "But while I have you here, I wanted to tell you how happy you've made me today. When you left, you broke *meine* heart, but today you have made everything right."

Matthew grunted.

Vater faced him. "Do you have something to say, *sohn*?"

With a scowl, he shook his head.

"Your sister was lost and now is found. We must rejoice in her return."

Her brother straightened and poked his finger in her direction. "She doesn't belong here and should leave." He stormed off.

"Matthew, come back here and apologize to your sister."

He took off in a run.

Her leaving and behavior had hurt him more than Dori could have imagined. She'd hurt many people when she left. Hadn't a clue so many people had cared.

Vater swung his gaze to her. "He will come around. Give him time."

She wasn't as sure. "I understand. I made bad choices. There will be consequences. Even so, I wouldn't want to be anyplace else."

"I'm glad to hear that."

"I need to speak to Eli. I'm going to go find him." As she walked off, she hoped he wasn't as hurt as her brother, but it didn't matter. She would earn back his trust if it took the rest of her life.

After church, Eli had escaped the crowd and now paced in the limited space of his forge. He grasped a foot-long iron rod. He couldn't work on a Sunday, and that frustrated him, but at least holding the cold metal helped calm him.

His heart had soared when Rainbow— Dori— *She* had gone up front to join. But why if she planned to leave? Had she done so for him, to prove he could trust her?

That wasn't necessary. He'd decided last night that it would hurt too much if she left again, and he would try his best to talk her into staying. But now that she'd joined, he feared it was for the wrong reasons. That would be worse than her leaving. He would never be certain she would stay. Each morning when he woke, he would wonder if she'd be gone.

He'd been selfish. *Gott* should be the reason she joined. Not him.

How could he be certain of her motives? If he asked her, that would be the same as accusing her of tainted motives. If he didn't, he would never know.

"Eli?"

He jumped at the sound of her voice and spun around. "Rain— Dor— Um." He frowned. "What are you doing here?"

"We came to see what you were up to. You aren't working on a Sunday, are you?"

She hadn't understood his question.

"*Ne.* I'm not working." He tapped the hunk of metal on his anvil. "I didn't mean what are you doing in *meine* forge. What are you doing here in the community? Here at church? Why bother coming?" He tossed the rod into the pile of scraps.

The clattering it made startled Tabitha, and she let out a whimper, then a cry.

He hurried over. "I'm sorry, *liebling.* I didn't think.

Shh, little one. It's all right." He put his large calloused hand on her head.

Tabitha calmed right down and turned toward his voice.

Rainbow Girl gazed up at him. "You have a way with her."

He kept his gaze focused on the babe. "I didn't do anything special."

"You didn't have to. She likes you being around." She shifted Tabitha in her arms. "You're missing out on the food. Are you coming back to the gathering?"

He removed his hand from the baby's head and shook his own. "I'm not…" He couldn't say he wasn't hungry, because that would be a lie. "I'll be out in a little bit." He stepped away.

Tabitha's head cocked in his direction.

"She always tries to find you when she hears you. Always responds to your voice. Somehow she's known from the start that you are a man to be trusted."

"Really?" He liked the idea and hoped her *mutter* trusted him, as well. He came forward again and held out his arms. "May I hold her?"

Rainbow Girl tilted her head. "You're asking?"

"Of course."

She smiled at him, and his insides went fuzzy. "Do you realize this is the first time you've asked to hold her?"

"I've held her many times." The more he spoke, the more Tabitha craned her head toward him.

"Each one of those times, I've either asked you, handed her to you or you've simply taken her out of *meine* arms."

"I have? I didn't realize. I'm sorry."

"Don't be sorry. Tabitha really likes you, and you are very comfortable holding her. Not all men are." She stepped closer and transferred the precious, little bundle into his arms.

Tabitha gazed up at him and one corner of her mouth pulled up into a smile, and a dimple showed on her right cheek. "She looks like you."

"Shall we go out and eat?"

He handed Tabitha back. "I have stuff to do in here." He spread his hands to indicate his workshop and forge.

"On Sunday?"

"Ne." He couldn't go on like this, not knowing her motive. *Gut* or bad, he needed to ask. He rubbed the back of his neck with his hand. "I was confused when you went up front and joined church. If you plan to leave, why join church? Why make everyone believe you're going to stay? Why get everyone's hopes up?" Why get his hopes up?

"I joined because I wanted to. I didn't know I wanted to until today. I *am* going to stay. I didn't want to when I came. Not from the beginning. I always planned to leave."

"So what are you saying? Are you keeping your options open?"

"Ne. I realized that this is where I belong. This, our community, is where I want to be. Here, standing in your forge with you, is where I want to be."

"So you're not going to leave?"

When she shook her head, his shoulders relaxed.

"I will be honest with you. Last night, I was. If I'd had someplace to go to, I would have. Since I didn't, I came to church one last time."

"So what made you decide to join if you were practically out the door?"

"I went back and forth on that decision. I realized *Gott* is the reason for everything. I kept thinking *meine* decision was between Craig or you. That whichever one of you wanted me, that's where I would be happy, but I realized it wasn't a choice between the two of you. Not even a choice between worlds, *English* or Amish, with or without either of you. It was to choose *Gott* or not. *Gott* is the reason for everything. I'm staying."

His hope soared. She'd chosen for the right reason.

"I can't tell you how happy that makes me."

"I know I've hurt you, but I want to prove to you that you can trust me. No matter how long that takes."

He didn't need any time. He trusted *Gott*, and that was what mattered. "From the start, I felt as though *Gott* brought you back for me. I didn't know if I could handle you leaving again. It was hard enough the first time when…"

"When what?"

He gazed straight into her eyes. "When I didn't care as much for you. But now…"

She took a step closer and tilted her head to look up at him. "But now what?"

"But now I care for you both. I want to be Tabitha's *vater*. Will you allow that?"

She gifted him with a smile. "What are you asking?"

Hadn't he been clear? "I love her as *meine* own. I will take *gut* care of her. What do you say?"

"And what about me?"

"You? You're her *mutter*."

Her smile didn't waver, as though she knew something he didn't. "But you want me to give *meine* daughter to you?"

"Ne— Ja— Ne." Now he understood. He hadn't asked her to be his wife, only asked if he could have her daughter. "Let me start over. Rain— Dor— I don't know what to call you anymore. You don't like *Dorcas.* You're no longer Rainbow Girl. Are you going to expect everyone to call you by your *Englisher* name, Dori?"

"Dori was *meine Englisher* name, but it doesn't suit me now that I'm Amish."

He liked the sound of that. She was Amish. "You could go by *Dorcas* again."

She scrunched up her nose. *"Dorcas* doesn't suit me either. I need something different for this new phase of *meine* life."

He smiled. "How about Dee Dee? Dorcas, Dori, *Dee Dee.*"

"I like that."

He put one hand on her shoulder and the other on Tabitha's head. "I don't want to lose either one of you. Dee Dee Bontrager, would you and your daughter become *meine* family—*meine* wife and daughter?"

"Ja. I— We would love to."

He cupped her face in his hands, leaned over his Rainbow Baby in her arms and kissed her.

For all her protests to the contrary, she—Dee Dee Bontrager, soon to be Hochstetler—had become Amish after all.

Epilogue

*Early August,
Five Years Later*

Dee Dee Hochstetler stood in her kitchen with her sister, Ruth Burkholder. She set empty glasses on a wooden serving tray along with the heaping plate of oatmeal cookies. Having been hunched over the table, Dee Dee jerked straight up and sucked in a breath. She placed a hand on her protruding belly. "Hey in there, settle down."

Ruth rushed to her side. "You aren't going into labor, are you?"

Dee Dee shook her head. "*Ne.* This one's just overactive. Doesn't give me a moment's peace."

"*Gut.* Because it's *meine* turn." Ruth picked up the pitchers of lemonade and iced tea. "You already have three little ones. I want to have *meine* baby before you have another one."

Like herself, Ruth was very pregnant.

Dee Dee lifted the tray. "You're welcome to have yours first. I want a chance to meet *meine* niece or nephew before this active one keeps me too busy." She exited out her kitchen door and held the screen open with her elbow for Ruth.

Eli hurried over in spite of having five-year-old Tabitha clinging to his back, three-and-a-half-year-old Sarah seated on one foot, holding on to his leg, and nearly two-year-old Evie sitting on the other. "Let me take that." He snatched the tray from her, and the glasses clinked.

"You're a bit occupied." Dee Dee loved seeing Eli playing with their daughters.

He glanced over his shoulder at one giggly girl, then at the two others on his feet. "*Ne.* They're no problem."

Dee Dee caressed her stomach. She hoped this one was a son for Eli. He never complained about having all girls so far, but she knew he longed for a son. Most men did. She'd worried when Sarah was born that he might favor his own daughter over Tabitha, but he showed no hint of that. Craig had eagerly signed away his parental rights, and Eli had officially adopted her.

With the girls still on each of his feet, Eli lumbered along toward the quilt stretched over a frame in the yard with the other three women around it, two as pregnant as Dee Dee and her sister.

Daniel Burkholder came over and relieved his wife of the beverage pitchers.

Dee Dee loved her life with Eli on their little farm. It had no crop fields, just a livestock pasture and a kitchen garden. Eli's ironwork business was thriving better than they'd ever dreamed of. Dee Dee took care of the business end of things so Eli could freely work in his blacksmith shop, creating beautiful and useful things.

Dr. Kathleen's and Deborah's husbands played in the yard with their three children.

Eli and Daniel made sure each of the four pregnant women as well as the bride-to-be had something to drink and a cookie before feeding the children and themselves.

Lowering her very pregnant body onto the chair in the circle, Dee Dee let out a huge sigh.

"You all right?" Dr. Kathleen asked.

"I'm fine. A part of me can't wait for this baby to be born so I can breathe and move around again."

"And the other part?" Deborah Burkholder asked.

"Wants it to stay in there forever. Once I have this little one in *meine* arms, I'm going to be too busy to do anything else, including sleep."

Deborah put her hand on her large belly. "I can't wait for mine to be born. I hope it's a girl this time."

It was going to be a race to see which of four out of five women around the quilt would give birth first. Dee Dee was pregnant with her fourth child, Dr. Kathleen Lambright with her third, Deborah Burkholder with number two and Dee Dee's sister, Ruth, pregnant with number one. All due imminently. It was anyone's guess who would go into labor first. Everyone secretly hoped Dr. Kathleen would be the last so she could deliver all their babies before she was unavailable.

Dee Dee gazed at the four ladies around the circle and felt a kindred spirit with them. Each had stepped sideways out of the traditional Amish mold. Dee Dee's sister, Ruth, had started an Amish blog to give the outside world an accurate view of the Amish people. Deborah Burkholder had been a model and earned a higher education degree in nutrition and homeopathic remedies. Kathleen Lambright had become a doctor, and her sister, Jessica, had earned her degree in business. Together, Jessica and Dee Dee helped other Amish make their businesses more effective. No more need to go outside their community for computer help.

Today, it was Jessica's quilt that had brought this group of rogue Amish women to Dee Dee's home. They were stitching the layers of her star quilt together for her upcoming wedding this fall.

Ruth gasped and dropped her lemonade in the grass.

Dee Dee reached for the toppled glass. "Don't worry. It didn't break." She patted her sister's arm.

Ruth's face had lost all its color.

"What's wrong?"

"How do I know if *meine* water broke?"

"Trust me, you'll know."

"Then I think it just did."

Dee Dee shifted her gaze across the circle. "Dr. Kathleen, it's time."

The doctor stood. "Let's get you inside the house."

"Not me. Ruth. Her water broke."

"Daniel!" the doctor called.

He rushed over.

"Help your wife into the house. Your child is on the way."

Dee Dee was relieved to turn her sister over to others. She put a hand on her aching back.

Eli with the three girls came up to her. "Are you all right? You're not in labor, are you?"

"I'm fine." But if the pain lanced across her back and wrapping around to her stomach was any indication, she was. Right now, she needed to focus on her sister.

By the end of the day, four baby boys had been born.

Dee Dee had managed to wait until after Ruth gave birth to have hers. The work and excitement had put Dr. Kathleen into labor with Deborah close on her heels. An influx of other women from the community left none of them without plenty of help. Each new *mutter* had been taken to her own house. Dee Dee's home sat quiet at one in the morning. She would cherish this rare moment of silence. She had nestled herself in the living room recliner to feed baby Abel, who now slept in her arms.

Eli came into the dimly lit room and knelt beside her. "How's he doing?"

"Great. He ate well. Are you happy to have a son?" Dee Dee knew she was.

"I am, but I wouldn't have minded to have another daughter. I love *meine* girls. All of them." He leaned forward and kissed Dee Dee on the mouth. "Let me take him. You go get some sleep." He scooped the little one into his big, strong arms.

She had the life she had always wanted. She stood, tiptoed and kissed her marvelous husband. *Gott* had blessed her in spite of her prodigal ways.

* * * * *

*If you loved this story,
check out the previous books
in Mary Davis's miniseries
Prodigal Daughters:*

Courting Her Amish Heart
Courting Her Secret Heart

Available now from Love Inspired!

Find more great reads at www.LoveInspired.com.

Dear Reader,

I hope you enjoyed the third book of the Prodigal Daughters series, featuring Amish women with nontraditional hopes and dreams.

I wanted to portray women who didn't follow the traditional path for an Amish. And what prodigal series would be complete without a true prodigal who turned her back on her way of life, her family and everything she knew? For this book, I wanted a young woman who looked very different from the Amish. But deep inside, she still held on to a few core Amish beliefs. I had to figure out what would drive someone so against the Amish way of life back into their midst.

Dori is dear to my heart because she had such an emptiness inside her that she was looking everywhere to fill. Finally, she found what she sought: *Gott*. Unlike Kathleen and Deborah, Dori isn't named for one of my wonderful sisters. But I did dedicate this book to my late son, Josh. He was my prodigal who found people fallible and God sufficient. If Josh had met Dori with her rainbow hair, he no doubt would have fallen in love with her.

Happy reading!

Blessings,
Mary

SPECIAL EXCERPT FROM

*After returning to his Amish community after losing his
job in the Englisch world, Aaron King isn't sure if he
wants to stay. But the more time he spends training a
horse with childhood friend Sally Stoltzfus, the more he
begins to believe this is exactly where he belongs.*

Read on for a sneak preview of
The Promised Amish Bride *by Marta Perry,*
available February 2019 from Love Inspired!

"Komm now, Aaron. I thought you might be ready to keep your
promise to me."

"Promise?" He looked at her blankly.

"You can't have forgotten. You promised you'd wait until I
grew up and then you'd marry me."

He stared at her, appalled for what seemed like forever until
he saw the laughter in her eyes. "Sally Stoltzfus, you've turned
into a threat to my sanity. What are you trying to do, scare me to
death?"

She gave a gurgle of laughter. "You looked a little bored with
the picnic. I thought I'd wake you up."

"Not bored," he said quickly. "Just…trying to find my way.
So you don't expect me to marry you. Anything else I can do
that's not so permanent?"

"As a matter of fact, there is. I want you to help me train Star."

So that was it. He frowned, trying to think of a way to refuse
that wouldn't hurt her feelings.

"You saw what Star is like," she went on without waiting for
an answer. "I've got to get him trained, and soon. And everyone
knows that you're the best there is with horses."

"I don't think everyone believes any such thing," he retorted.
"They don't know me well enough anymore."

She waved that away. "You've been working with horses

while you were gone. And Zeb always says you were born with the gift."

"Onkel Zeb might be a little bit prejudiced," he said, trying to organize his thoughts. There was no real reason he couldn't help her out, except that it seemed like a commitment, and he didn't intend to tie himself anywhere, not now.

"You can't deny that Star needs help, can you?" Her laughing gaze invited him to share her memory of the previous day.

"He needs help all right, but I don't quite see the point. Can't you use the family buggy when you need it?" He suspected that if he didn't come up with a good reason, he'd find himself working with that flighty gelding.

Her face grew serious suddenly. "As long as I do that, I'm depending on someone else. I want to make my own decisions about when and where I'm going. I'd like to be a bit independent, at least in that. I thought you were the one person who might understand."

That hit him right where he lived. He did understand— that was the trouble. He understood too well, and it made him vulnerable where Sally was concerned. He fumbled for words. "I'd like to help. But I don't know how long I'll be here and—"

"That doesn't matter." Seeing her face change was like watching the sun come out. "I'll take whatever time you can spare. Denke, Aaron. I'm wonderful glad."

He started to say that his words hadn't been a yes, but before he could, Sally had grabbed his hand and every thought flew right out of his head.

It was just like her catching hold of Onkel Zeb's arm, he tried to tell himself. But it didn't work. When she touched him, something seemed to light between them like a spark arcing from one terminal to another. He felt it right down to his toes, and he knew in that instant that he was in trouble.

Don't miss
The Promised Amish Bride *by Marta Perry,*
available February 2019 wherever
Love Inspired® *books and ebooks are sold.*

www.LoveInspired.com

Love Inspired®

Inspirational Romance to Warm Your Heart and Soul

Join our social communities to connect with other readers who share your love!

Sign up for the Love Inspired newsletter at **www.LoveInspired.com** to be the first to find out about upcoming titles, special promotions and exclusive content.

CONNECT WITH US AT:

Facebook.com/groups/HarlequinConnection

 Facebook.com/LoveInspiredBooks

 Twitter.com/LoveInspiredBks

LISOCIAL2018

lover in you!

Earn points on your purchase of new Harlequin books from participating retailers.

Turn your points into **FREE BOOKS** of your choice!

Join for FREE today at
www.HarlequinMyRewards.com.

Harlequin My Rewards is a free program (no fees) without any commitments or obligations.

MYR18